THE DUKE'S SHOTGUN WEDDING

Scandalous House of Calydon

THE DUKE'S SHOTGUN WEDDING

Scandalous House of Calydon

STACY REID

Entangled Publishing, LLC
2614 South Timberline Road
Suite 109
Fort Collins, CO 80525
Visit our website at www.entangledpublishing.com.

Scandalous is an imprint of Entangled Publishing, LLC.

Edited by Nina Bruhns
Cover design by Erin Dameron-Hill
Cover art from Period Images, Shutterstock, and iStock

Manufactured in the United States of America

First Edition April 2014

SCANDALOUS

To my love, my heart, Dusean Nelson. Without your love, your support, I am incomplete.

Chapter One

London
November 1882

Lady Jocelyn Rathbourne's hand did not waver as she pointed the derringer at the Duke of Calydon. Eyes that were the color of winter blue, colder than the wind that whistled through the open windows, stared at her penetratingly. Jocelyn gritted her teeth and desperately hoped that he did not hear the pounding of her heart, or sensed her fear. He was reputed to be ruthless, and have one of the shrewdest minds in all London. But then, Jocelyn's papa had always called her his little Napoleon.

Long elegant fingers coolly caressed the card that she had presented to his butler to gain entrance, and those ice-blue eyes flicked to the note she had written. "I must assume that the house and name on this card are as fabricated as this dire situation your note hinted at?"

Jocelyn flushed as the husky rasp of his voice stirred deep within her. She was taken aback by how sinfully attractive he was.

She squinted at him as rage flared through her, scorching in its intensity. She was not about to be taken in by the man. Not ever again by a pretty face and prettier lies. Not that she could call the duke pretty. He was more raw and masculine, possibly handsome—if not for the rapier scar that had flayed his left cheek. But he was certainly compelling with his midnight black hair and mesmerizing eyes. His appearance was everything a powerful duke's should be as he sat behind his massive oak desk intricately carved with designs of dragons—dark, sensual, handsome, with just a hint of danger.

She gave an involuntary shiver, then scowled as his lips turned up as he noted her body's reaction. Thank goodness he could not see past her veil.

"My name is most certainly not fabricated, Your Grace," she said, and straightened her stance. "I am Lady Jocelyn, the daughter of the Earl of Waverham, and your brother has perpetrated the most heinous crimes upon my person and must be brought to justice!"

He relaxed in his chair as if she were not a serious threat. She gritted her teeth and ignored the cold flint that entered his eyes as she raised the gun a little higher, in line with his chest.

"Well, in that case, please take a seat." He gestured at the high-backed chair she was standing next to. His expression didn't waver.

She didn't want to give him the satisfaction of following his orders. But her knees were shaking so badly she thought it might be best. She sat gingerly on the edge of the chair.

"Now. What heinous crime has Anthony perpetrated that has you invading my country home and committing a crime that will certainly see you to the gallows?" His voice had gone flat and hard.

She leaned forward and slapped a copy of the London

Gazette on his oak desk, sending it skidding across the polished surface, tumbling the inkwell. "The society page reports his engagement to Miss Phillipa Peppiwell of the Boston Peppiwells." Jocelyn's lips curled in derision as she spat the woman's name at him like it was one of her bullets.

"And this distresses you…how?"

Her hands wavered slightly as the duke leaned forward, resting his chin in his hands, studying her as if she were a fascinating bug.

She drew herself up. "He seduced me!"

The crackling of the fireplace hushed as if waiting for an explosion, but her hand did not waver. Not even when the elegant royal blue drapes billowed under a sharp gust of the winter wind.

"I beg your pardon?" His voice was so low she was not sure if he'd really spoken, or if she'd simply imagined a response. He gazed steadily at her, his expression betraying not the slightest flicker of reaction.

She swallowed. "He seduced me, promised me marriage, and even gave me this as a token of his affection. An *engagement* token."

She sent the locket skidding across the desk to be halted by a finger. The chain of the necklace slid through his hands slowly. A muscle ticked in his forehead as he glanced at the golden locket.

"Anthony gifted this to you?" His voice was chillingly polite, but his eyes had gone from wintery to glacial as he tracked her movements, missing nothing.

"Yes, as a promise of his commitment to me," she assured him. "Yet now I read that he is engaged to be married in fewer than three weeks." She shifted in the high-backed chair, straining to keep her hand from trembling as she aimed the derringer.

He cocked his head as he considered her, and she

desperately wished to have just an inkling of his thoughts.

"Could this, by chance, be a desperate ploy by the impoverished Earl of Waverham?"

Jocelyn flinched at the soft question and forced herself to hold steady under the ruthless intelligence that shone in his eyes as he studied her carefully. Again she was grateful her eyes were covered by the veil. Her hair was also hidden, completely stuffed under her top hat, giving her partial anonymity, albeit useless since she'd told him her name. She fought not to squirm under his stare. "My father might be impoverished, Your Grace, but he does not plot, nor is he desperate," she said, lifting the gun for a better aim. "Is this *your* desperate ploy—to lay the abominable behavior of your brother at my father's door step?"

His brows flickered.

"Despite my weapon's fragile appearance, Your Grace, it is not easy to aim a derringer at a man this long. My hand tires…I may accidentally pull the trigger."

"Ah, so it is not your intention to shoot me, Miss Rathbourne?"

She ignored the eyes that roved over her. "It's *Lady* Rathbourne. And most assuredly, my intention to shoot you is genuine, if I do not receive justice. I would hate for my shot to be accidental. It will be done very deliberately when I choose to fire."

The duke unlocked his hands from under his chin and leaned back in his chair. He drummed his fingers on his desk with a *click clack* sound, possibly hoping to unnerve her as he studied her. She had to admit she was slightly intimidated by the glare from his eyes.

Despite being an Earl's daughter, due to their dire financial straits she had not received the chance to have her season, her foray into society. Today was the first she'd laid eyes on the formidable duke, knowing him only by reputation and Anthony's recounts.

"Are you with child?" he asked evenly.

She spluttered, a wave of heat blossoming on her entire body at his unexpected question. Mortified, she gazed at his expressionless face, uncertain how to answer.

"A seduction does not necessarily result in a child, Your Grace." At the slow raise of his eyebrows, she hazarded a guess that what Anthony had told her was correct. "As you are a man of the world, I am sure you are aware that the outcome of a child can be prevented?" She posed the question, and her lips tightened in a moue as she awaited his answer with heart pounding.

"You may lower your weapon, Miss Rathbourne. And do not presume to correct me of your title, as a *lady* would not barge into my home under false pretense and threaten me at the point of a gun." His fingers halted their drumming. "Indeed, I am uncertain as to what you require of me."

Her eyes narrowed at the insult of him referring to her as *Miss*. A scathing reply formed on her lips, but she had to remind herself of what her aim was. After a brief hesitation, she lowered her arms, but she did it slowly, and rested the derringer in her lap, continuing to point it directly at him. For some unfathomable reason, she liked the amused twitch of his mouth as his wintry gaze thawed. He shifted, his jacket stretching over his very broad shoulders. His blue waistcoat was the finest she had ever seen.

"I have no pretenses, Your Grace, and everything I said in my note is the absolute truth."

He looked skeptical. "Your note claimed a dire situation of grave misfortune that threatens scandal and *death* for my family—namely my wicked brother Anthony Williamson Thornton."

"Despite what polite society would have many believe, a seduction does not have only one perpetrator, Miss

Rathbourne. Now, let's get down to business. What is it you want? Money? A house?"

Affront flared through Jocelyn and she raised her weapon with such speed he froze in the act of opening his top drawer.

"How *dare* you!" She breathed deeply to contain the rage that burned through her. "Do you not have a sister enjoying her first season? If a cad had used her, enticing her with promises of love and marriage, then abandoned her, what recompense would *you* demand? Money? A house? A duel? Or a marriage?"

"Only death would suffice."

She flinched at his unwavering response, the derringer jerking in her clasp. "I do not desire Anthony's death." Her stomach churned at the mere thought of it. "It discredits you to speak so easily of your brother's demise."

Once more, amusement twisted his sensual mouth, infuriating her.

"I spoke to the demise of a hypothetical cad who had seduced and abandoned my sister. Not of my brother, Miss Rathbourne."

"But it was your *brother* who seduced and abandoned me. I demand marriage!" she said, trying to keep her voice from trembling.

"Request denied."

She felt her back go ramrod straight and she vibrated with rage. "I beg your pardon?"

He held up a hand. "I do not deliberately stoke your scorned woman's wrath, but I am afraid Anthony is already married."

She darted a gaze to the *Gazette* with a frown. "You lie!"

The smile that twisted his lips at her slander was not one of amusement.

She flushed and swallowed. *No*. It couldn't be true. "I—"

"Let me be clear. Money is all that will be offered. Do

I believe my brother seduced you? Frankly, yes. Only a madwoman would storm my estate with such an elaborate story that can be so easily verified. And make no mistake, it will be verified." The muscle in his forehead ticked again. "However, Anthony and Miss Peppiwell had the brilliant notion to abscond to Gretna Green with a special license two weeks past. Ergo, they are now married and she may be enceinte. Thus the reaffirmation of vows in three weeks that will appear to polite society as their actual marriage."

Jocelyn blanched, lowering the gun as her mind sifted through her options with dizzying speed. Despair made her voice hoarse when she responded. "I will need proof."

It was the Duke of Calydon's turn to throw a paper onto his desk, one he pulled from the top drawer. She reached for it, and gasped as she read the document. Dear God, it was true. *Anthony was married*. Pain squeezed her chest tight and her hands trembled as she lowered the paper. She slid it back across the desk with infinite slowness.

"One hundred thousand pounds is my first and final offer." He rose from his chair and stalked around the desk toward her. She scrambled up from her seat and her reticule fell from her lap, spilling its contents on the lavender Aubusson carpet.

"Come no farther!" she cried, the words echoing off the library walls. She pressed her back against the bookshelves that lined them and stared at him with wide eyes. She did not like the duke's smile as he detoured to the sideboard and poured ruby liquor from a decanter into two glasses.

The crumbled ruin that was her father's estate flashed in her head. A hundred thousand pounds would put him on the path of removing the unrelenting burden of debt that was entailed with his property, and possibly give him a fighting chance.

She almost took it.

But then the voices of her sisters rushed in, crowding her

mind.

Do you think I will ever have a season, Jocelyn? Her beautiful younger sister Victoria.

I wish not to be so cold all the time, but I think I would prefer to have pretty dresses like Lady Elizabeth. Don't you wish for pretty things, Jocelyn? Her twelve year old sister Emily, more bookish and enraptured by Latin, Plutarch, and Socrates—as was Jocelyn—but sometimes wholly feminine in her desire for dresses and pretty trinkets.

Jocelyn's throat tightened as the voices that affected her most blared in her head. *I wish for warm milk on Christmas morning. Loevnia says every Christmas her mama and papa give her presents under a Christmas tree. They eat roast duckling! Pudding! And Christmas punch! Yum! If we could only have such things…* The eight year old twins Emma and William had danced together as they fantasized, yet Emma's voice had rung hollow for someone so young. But it was William's sad smile as he said, *I would be so happy if you were warm, Emma*, which had decided everything for Jocelyn.

The raise of the derringer to Calydon's chest was slow and deliberate, as was the cool smoothness of her voice as she said, "If Anthony is unavailable for marriage, Your Grace, an offer from you will do. That is the only thing that can atone for your brother's reprehensible conduct."

Chapter Two

Ah, yes. She would do.

Sebastian Jackson Thornton, the twelfth Duke of Calydon, Marquess of Hastings, and Earl of Blaydon had decided on Lady Jocelyn Rathbourne the instant she drew the derringer from her reticule and pointed it at him so determinedly. Or it could have been when his butler Thomas announced her entry. Her walk had been militant yet provocative and graceful, stirring something that had withered to a cold nothing over the years. He doubted those qualities were natural, as chits like her were trained from the schoolroom how to walk, talk, and entice a man to marriage.

Even though, Sebastian had to admit, she did not appear like many of the simpering misses and ladies of the *ton* who thought they had only to bat an eyelash and wield their fan to be captivating.

"Marriage?" he asked blandly, as his eyes tracked the pulse that beat so frantically at her throat.

He held out the glass of sherry. "Drink," he commanded, expecting her to obey without question. He suppressed an impulse to smile as her lips flattened, and from the slight spasm of her jaw he surmised she was gritting her teeth. She would make a poor gambler.

He wondered at her eyes—their color and shape. The dark veil that covered them was a source of irritation he meant to remedy. Her hand trembled as she pressed her back closer into the shelves that lined his library walls, filled with thousands of books and tomes. He hoped her bravado was not failing her. It would not do for him to turn around and offer marriage so easily.

"Yes, marriage." Her voice was a hiss as she straightened her spine and took a tentative step forward. "And I do not desire refreshment."

Ah, there it was. The spirit that had stoked his intrigue, the sheer boldness that had rushed from her as she confronted him with Anthony's folly, so different from the simpering flowers the mamas of the *ton* had been throwing in his path over the years. She vibrated with passion and fire.

"Very well."

Her gaze slashed from his to the glass of sherry he placed on the desk. His chuckle when it rumbled from his throat surprised even him. The unthinkable deed that he had been contemplating with part rage and sometimes icy detachment suddenly seemed intriguing as he studied her. Slowly, he closed the distance between them.

"Come no farther!"

He halted inches from her, the barrel tip of the derringer brushing against his waistcoat. He ignored her gasp as he reached out deliberately and drew the hat from her head.

"What are you doing?" she demanded, grabbing for it. He held it behind his back.

He liked that her voice did not lose its husky timber even though she appeared rattled, so unlike the high-pitched nasal tone of the many debutantes of the summer season.

He was even more relieved that her voice was not pure throaty seductiveness, or else his disgust would have been instant. Stripped of its veil, her delicate face had blushed crimson, and her gray eyes were like saucers. He feared she may be in danger of fainting.

"It is normal, Miss Rathbourne, for a man to fully gaze upon his intended before committing to marriage, especially under such unorthodox circumstances."

She took several breaths and lowered the weapon slightly, in line with his waist. He circled her neck with his hand, his thumb teasing the pulse that fluttered at her throat. Her tongue peeked out and moistened her lips. His nostril flared, but he ruthlessly ignored the sudden desire that burned him. She had dressed for their meeting in her riding habit: a green, high-collared shirt with matching skirts that molded her petite but voluptuous figure. From the nerve-racking tutelage he had received from his sister, Constance, about the current season's fashion, Sebastian determined that she was wearing last season's habit.

She inhaled sharply as he stepped in close enough to her that she was forced to lower her weapon completely or shoot him. Her eyes widened even further, and Sebastian realized he'd done her an injustice when he'd thought of them as merely gray. They were the color of storm clouds, full and raging with emotion.

"Your Grace, you presume too much!"

"Do I?" Sebastian chuckled as the click of the gun echoed like the crack of a whip. "Brave little thing, aren't you?"

"You will address me as Lady Jocelyn." She lifted the derringer again, and pressed it to his ribs. "Unhand me, and summon your solicitor at once. I require him to procure a special license and prepare our marriage contract."

"Ah." He reached past her and set her hat and veil on the bookshelf. "In that case, I fear I must insist on first sampling the wares you so boldly offer, Miss…*Lady* Rathbourne."

She froze. "*Sample?* I am not a common doxy!"

"No you are not…nor are you a lady." He traced his thumb along her jaw. "I have yet to figure out what you are, Jocelyn."

"Oomph—"

He swallowed her reply in a kiss, an action meant to shock the sensibilities she obviously possessed. But instead, it completely floored him.

The flavor of her lips was like the finest wine, the texture sublime, and her taste could intoxicate even the most jaded rake. She went rigid against him. He clasped her face with both hands and tilted her back, sinking in for a more thorough kiss. She shuddered, and parted her lips on a soft gasp which he took immediate advantage of, dipping his tongue into heaven.

The stab of his own arousal stunned him, yet what he tasted from her infuriated him, sending rage through his blood like poison.

For he tasted innocence.

It was there in the hesitant dart of her tongue as it met his, in the soft moan, the hand that fluttered to his shoulder, clasping him tightly as he deepened the kiss, and her shiver as he slanted his lips over hers. But it was the guileless hunger she responded with that bespoke her innocence. There was no artifice, no seduction…and no expertise behind her natural response. It was pure and unguarded, and it drew him under as nothing else could.

He kissed her with scorching proficiency, drawing her pleasure as an artist with a brush. His tongue plunged into the warm recess of her mouth, tasting nectar, eliciting a fractured moan. His hunger grew, and he licked and engaged her tongue in a feast of the senses. Her body arched, and he groaned as her moans roused the full length of his cock. Too much, and too soon for the innocence he tasted, for as he molded her body to his, curving her shape and pillowing her breast to his chest, she tore her mouth from his. Horrified by his boldness, or by her own response, he wasn't certain. But he could guess.

"How *dare* you!" she choked out.

The storm clouds of her eyes appeared about to crack, unleashing torrents of rage. Her lips glistened, the high flush on her cheeks spread to her neck and lower, her petite frame held taut with outrage.

She was magnificent in her fury.

. . .

"You take liberties, Your Grace! Your actions are of an unspeakable cad!" Jocelyn spluttered, and darted sideways away from Calydon, lest she shoot him and unravel all that she had plotted for.

He tilted his head and regarded her. "It seems your shrewish tongue is the offset to such angelic beauty, Lady Jocelyn."

"And you are a libertine!" She had not been in his library thirty minutes and he had accosted her. Her hands trembled and her heart pounded in shock.

Mostly at the startling pleasure of his kiss.

His actions had surprised her so much she had responded with a wantonness not in her nature. How had he wrought such a change in her?

The man was more dangerous than she'd ever imagined.

Heat burned in her entire body as she remembered how the duke had crushed her to him and plundered her mouth as though he had every right.

With an unreadable mien, he turned to watch her, graceful and panther-like in his movements. Her hand itched to shoot him for his arrogance, so much so that she clasped both hands over the derringer in fear she might actually pull the trigger.

His brows arched at her action. "Do you still intend to shoot me, Lady Rathbourne?" he drawled, seemingly unconcerned that she held a gun in her shaking hand.

"I can see where Anthony received his propensity for disgraceful, ungentlemanly behavior."

His lip curled. "You mistook me for a gentleman? How naïve. For I am still trying to determine if I will take you before you leave."

She could only gape at him in stupefied amazement. She searched his face, and what she saw shook her to the core. Her hand stilled, and all tremors left her body as her mind endeavored to understand.

He was coldly furious.

She was sure of it. The curve of his lips, and the ease with which he leaned against his oak desk suggested otherwise. But his eyes gave him away. They burned with an intensity she did not understand. *She* was the wronged party, not him.

She belatedly realized that Calydon was nothing like Anthony, or the few other noblemen who had graced her home in Lincolnshire. He was not like the earnest suitors her father maneuvered her way hoping they would be ensnared by her beauty and title despite the lack of a dowry. This man was not amiable, easily spoken, nor, indeed, a gentleman. He would not be led nor easily deceived. He was a lord, through and through.

Rich, powerful, and ruthless, and Jocelyn feared she was far out of her league, even if her papa claimed her Napoleonic mind had no match.

Restrained strength emanated from him, and a dark sensuality stamped his features. Despite the smile that teased his lips, his eyes remained cold, distant, and aloof.

She rocked back on her heels, and tipped her head to search his face. His reputation for shrewdness and ruthlessness extended to more than business acumen. Apparently it was well-earned. She was not dealing with a rich fop of the revered *ton* as she had believed.

"You are angry," she observed, her heart pounding.

She watched his face for signs that she may be wrong. And did her best to block what he had said about taking her. Visions of true ruin had been pummeling her since he'd uttered those threatening words. If he did, she would be more than impoverished, she would be disgraced and cast from society. If not worse. Should he decide to force her, she doubted she could shoot him and remain a free woman. Images of her swinging from the gallows had her paling.

"Because I detest liars." His voice whipped contempt.

Jocelyn swept down her lashes, shuttering her gaze. "I am telling the truth." In all that mattered…

"Anthony did *not* seduce you. And if so, he did a piss poor job at it."

Her eyes flew open at his crude remarks. "You persist in thinking me a simpleton! I demand satisfaction. I swear on my honor that your brother took liberties and promised me marriage."

She did not fidget under his cold assessment, despite the riotous emotions that boiled inside her.

"Women have no honor." His tone was positively glacial, devoid of anything but disdain.

She struggled for a reply, but could say nothing under the judgment that lashed out from his eyes. Fire burned in her cheeks.

"Ah, she blushes. Mortification at being revealed?"

"Blushing is the color of virtue, Your Grace," she snapped.

"A gun-toting woman who quotes the philosopher Diogenes. Tell me, Lady Rathbourne, what other talents lie beneath such a beautiful face and glorious body? Do you paint water colors or play the pianoforte, perhaps?"

She cursed the weakness that filled her limbs as he slowly

perused the length of her, from the tendrils of curls on her forehead, over her breasts, where he lingered a moment, then all the way down to her black boots.

She drew herself up and met his derision with pride. "No. But I do read and write in fluent English, French, and Latin. I don't know all the great philosophers, only those who had something interesting to say. I am apt in managing a household, and have served as both chatelaine and steward for my father's estate for years. I swim, I ride, and I hunt. And I shoot very, very well."

He strolled to the bell and rang it, ignoring her passionate outburst. The butler instantly appeared, as if he had been stationed outside the door all along.

She gaped in humiliation.

The butler bowed. "Yes, Your Grace?"

"Summon the vicar," Calydon ordered. "And have the cook prepare luncheon for me and my future duchess."

The room swam around Jocelyn at his pronouncement. She dropped abruptly onto the chair and reached for the glass of sherry on his desk. She drank it in three unladylike gulps.

She had to admire the butler's aplomb. He betrayed neither dismay nor pleasure at the duke's announcement. "Yes, Your Grace." He bowed again, and exited.

She took a steadying breath. "Your Grace, I—"

"Sebastian, please. Now we are on intimate terms, let's dispense with the titles, Jocelyn."

A shiver went through her at the way he said her name, rolling it slowly over his tongue as if tasting and savoring the syllables. She frowned, disoriented and overwhelmed. He was so mercurial. She knew rage had held him in its grip a few moments ago, darkening his eyes to deep blue. Now he was smiling at her with lazy sensuality, all trace of rage suppressed behind shuttered eyes.

"You are marrying me?" She was still disbelieving of

what she'd heard.

"Was that not your demand? I cannot give you the satisfaction of Anthony's hand, nor can I meet you on the field of honor at dawn. And I certainly do not wish to be shot in my own library. I thought you said I would do?"

"I…I am merely startled by the ease of your capitulation, Your Gr…Sebastian. I feared I would at least have to shoot you in the arm for my intentions not to be doubted." She glanced uncertainly at the closed door. "You sent for the vicar."

"Yes…he will marry us upon his arrival."

Jocelyn laughed, the sound thin and high. "You jest, I'm sure."

"Do I detect unwillingness? Is there a chance I mistook your meaning when you demanded satisfaction?"

She surged to her feet. "No, you did not."

She paced the library in a daze unable to stay still. "The scandal of wedding so quickly without my family present, or a courting period of a few weeks at least—"

"Denied."

"I beg your pardon?" She plucked up her veil and top hat, and clutched them to her chest.

"I do not bow to the conventions of society, Jocelyn. Nor did I imagine that you did, after the way you stormed my estate waving your derringer."

Her feet sank into the thick carpet as she resumed pacing. The duke leaned against the bookshelf and watched her.

"I cannot credit that you would have us wed so soon. It's impossible. The banns will need to be read and—"

"I will procure a special license and we will wed tomorrow morning at nine."

She gaped at him. "I do not think it possible to obtain a license so soon, Sebastian."

"I am the Duke of Calydon. It will be done."

She blinked at him owlishly, unsure if she could even scoff at his arrogance.

A slow, devastating smile slashed his features and she swallowed at the strange flutter it caused inside her.

"Are you at least twenty-one, Jocelyn?"

"Yes"

"Then I will have my solicitor visit Doctor's Common and procure a special license for us."

A disconcerting thrill went through Jocelyn at his words. He was willing to marry her.

Disbelief and a deep excitement unfurled within her. She stopped her pacing abruptly, staring at him with wide eyes. He prowled over to her as myriad emotions tumbled through her—doubt, fear, relief, followed by unguarded joy. Her family was saved.

But it didn't take long for the fear and uncertainty to return. Could she really do this? "I…"

"Yes, Jocelyn?"

"My father will object to such a short notice. I fear he may—"

"You will spend the night here at Sherring Cross and we will wed in the morning. There is no need for you to return home to face his objections."

Jocelyn stared at him, scandalized. She had not forgotten what he'd said about taking her. Even if he provided a paragon with the most virtuous of sensibilities as a chaperon, she would not spend a night under his roof. "Please disabuse yourself of such a ludicrous notion. I have a cousin who resides in Cringleford. I could visit her, and send a note informing my father of my decision," she ventured carefully.

"Does that mean you consent to marrying me tomorrow?"

She had no choice. She must, for her sisters. To give them all a chance at happiness. That had been the plan all along.

Taking a deep breath, she said the most momentous words

of her life. "Yes, I will marry you tomorrow, Your Grace."

She didn't dare analyze the shadow of primitive satisfaction that swept across his face.

Nor did she have time, since he quickly angled his head down, gently fitting his lips against hers, sealing their agreement.

And as she melted into his too-tempting kiss, she just hoped those words would not also prove the most calamitous of her life.

Chapter Three

Jocelyn's capitulation had ignited a fire in Sebastian's cock and he could still taste her on his tongue. After taking luncheon with her and conferring with his lawyer, he had used the remainder of the day to draft their marriage contract. He'd spent the night restless, wondering if she would return to Sherring Cross. This morning, he dared not analyze the feeling of pleasure and satisfaction that permeated every cell in his body when his butler announced her promptly at eight o'clock.

She was dressed in her freshly laundered riding habit with her hair pulled back in a severe bun. Sebastian thought she looked delectable.

She graciously consented to break her fast with him despite her apparent nervousness. Conversation for the following hour was very stilted, but Sebastian did not mind. He felt contented observing her and envisioning the upcoming night.

He suppressed a flare of need as he watched her eat the last morsel on her plate. She darted her tongue to capture a crumble of cake from the corner of her mouth. Her lips had a lush sexuality, and he swallowed a groan at the mental image of her tongue caressing his thick shaft. He doubted he'd ever anticipated being deep inside someone as he had her.

The emotions that stirred as he'd watched her for the past hour were not welcome. And yet, her boldness pulled him, and the mirrored need in her gaze intrigued him as she watched him covertly and with a soft hunger. He wasn't given to fanciful notions, but if he was not careful, he could find himself steadily craving her. A state he would never welcome.

Despite her innocence, given her easy capitulation to his brother's charms, Sebastian fully expected her to be unfaithful in marriage. Wasn't that what women did? They couldn't be trusted. He'd learned that the hard way from the two women he had loved and given his trust.

A savage surge of denial filled him at the thought that she might betray him to such an extent. His fingers clenched tight around his knife. He forced himself to release it, and leaned back in his chair. He would not suffer disloyalty or betrayal from her.

Her nervousness grew notably when his butler announced the vicar's arrival. Her gaze flitted around the room, glancing everywhere but at him.

He rose and sauntered toward her, enjoying her discomfort. Next time, perhaps she would be more cautious in her demands.

"Come. The vicar awaits us in the library." She scraped back her chair and came to her feet without waiting for him to assist her. She walked before him with short, easy strides, graceful yet determined, and the rounded curve of her backside had arousal teasing him once more. Thrusting his hands in his trouser pockets he wondered how best to deal with her. He knew full well she was only marrying him for his wealth. Not that he cared. He did not know if there had ever been a time when marriage had been about something other than money.

A sensual smile curved his lips. Though, indeed, marriage did have certain other benefits. He would ensure the lady had no time even to think of taking a lover, if that was her wont. He would keep her—and himself—well pleasured, day and night, riding her long, slow, and deep. If she then still had the withal to find a lover, he would either tip his hat to her or banish her.

She swept into the parlor and halted when she saw the two young ladies who waited. She glanced at him.

"These are Vicar Primrose's wife and daughter, Miss Alicia and Mrs. Felicity Primrose. They are our witnesses," he explained.

They rose to their feet, twin blond heads bobbing to greet them.

Jocelyn nodded mutely in acknowledgement, and he signaled the baffled vicar to begin.

He wondered fleetingly if he should halt the proceedings to grant her a courtship period and a wedding that befitted a duchess. Was he denying her a dream that he could easily accede to? Constance, his sister, reminded him every so often that it was an atrocity not to be married in a wedding gown fashioned by Worth from Paris. But he dismissed the notion immediately. This was a business arrangement. She wanted his money, and he wanted an heir. Dreams didn't enter into it.

The vicar cleared his throat and asked them to face each other. Satisfaction rushed through Sebastian when she squared her shoulders, lifted her chin a notch, and met his eyes unflinchingly.

As the vicar's voice droned on, he only partially listened to the words of affirmation and commitment. He responded when needed, a smile quirking his lips whenever he noted the wild fluttering at Jocelyn's throat that belied her serene expression. He couldn't help but admire her aplomb.

"Your Grace, the ring."

He withdrew it from his pocket and her hand shook when he slid the turquoise encrusted, rose-cut diamond ring on her finger. He could feel her surprise at it, no doubt wondering how he had come to procure such a beautiful ring so quickly.

A light sheen of disbelief then glazed her eyes as he tightened his fingers on hers, and said, "I thee wed, Jocelyn Virginia Charlotte Rathbourne."

Vicar Primrose asked her to repeat her vows. She complied, voice smooth and sure, holding his eyes captive the entire time.

The final words of the vicar binding them together resounded through the library. "Those whom God hath joined together, let no man put asunder."

Gratified, he listened to the vicar pronounce them man and wife. That had gone better than expected.

"Lady Calydon," he drawled, and slid his left arm about her waist drawing her close. He took her mouth with deliberate gentleness, aware of their audience. Her lips parted, and her taste, hot and sweet, sank into him. And slowly the kiss became deeper, hungrier. Only the discomfited squeaks of the vicar's wife and daughter pulled him from his bride.

He lifted his head, drinking in her beauty, anticipating the upcoming night. A blush reddened her cheeks, but her eyes glittered with heat. He felt like he was holding fire in his arms, and he wanted her with a ferocity that stunned him.

Not good. This was the way of folly. The path to losing one's heart, only to have it broken.

He stepped away from her, hardening himself against such treacherous emotions. She was a means to an heir, and a willing body to sate his needs, nothing more.

• • •

She was the Duchess of Calydon.

The lush countryside, the fresh bite of air did nothing to soothe Jocelyn's shattered nerves. She was still a little confused at what had happened in the library. The powerful Duke of Calydon had married her.

Her heart thumped in fright as she wondered for a moment if the marriage was legitimate, or if he had somehow seized a winning hand about which she knew nothing. She dismissed the notion as a product of the stress of the day. What could that possibly serve him?

When she had demanded marriage from him, it had been sheer recklessness that had driven her—and the bitter taste of failure. Never had she expected Sebastian to summon the vicar and actually wed her. She had been hoping to drive a harder bargain and have him offer two hundred thousand pounds. She still could not believe she went along with a marriage. In his many recounts of his brother, Anthony had repeatedly stressed how much the duke hated scandal, and how withdrawn he was from the glittering throng of society. Jocelyn had prayed for strength and hoped on that account he would affiance her to Anthony. She had also logically realized he would most likely offer monetary compensation in lieu of that, but while making the cold morning trip from Lincolnshire to his ducal estate in Norfolk, Jocelyn had been quite determined to secure marriage—to Anthony. Her family needed more than money. She needed Anthony's connections, a sponsor into society, if she had any hopes of giving her three sisters a semblance of a future away from the genteel poverty they had all been living in.

But to Calydon himself? The thought had never entered her mind. Not until the moment it had blurted out of her mouth. Last night she had visited her cousin, Rosamund, in Cringleford, and it had been difficult for her to partake in conversation and tea. She'd felt certain he was playing some cruel jest and had braced herself for disappointment when she arrived at Sherring Cross this morning. She'd been both elated and scared witless that he really intended to wed her.

The elegant Calydon chaise rumbled and rocked along the rough country path, the horses' whinnying jarring her from her thoughts. The carriage was pulled by a magnificent team of six. She knew the duke owned one of the finest stud farms in England, and the sleek, powerful grace of his horses mesmerized her. She leaned forward, peering out the windows as her home—*former* home—came into view. As usual, her breath caught at its majestic grace, and a smile pure and joyous came to her face for the first time in days.

Somehow, she really had done it!

Not only was her family truly saved, but her childhood home had been saved, as well.

Even though a grand manor with sixty seven rooms, Stonehaven, with its rustic design, paled in comparison to the duke's country home. The grounds of Sherring Cross, Sebastian's palatial estate, were stunning. The rolling lawns, the rings of gardens, and the several lakes her carriage had rumbled past had taken her breath. The land had been softly dotted with snow, and the many gardens made up of blood-red roses against the snowy backdrop had made Jocelyn feel as if she were in a fairytale land. But it was the sheer size of the estate that had amazed her. Anthony had boasted it had one hundred and fifty rooms and sat on over forty thousand acres of land.

And she would be its duchess.

Jocelyn hugged herself and grinned. And refused to let the thought that tonight she must dance to Sebastian's tune mar her joy.

I am looking forward to our wedding night.

She swallowed, recalling the parting words he had whispered against her lips. She had been so nervous when the vicar had made the final pronouncement that bound them together for life. For some reason she had pictured Sebastian whisking her off and ravishing her right then and there. She had been so relieved when he acquiesced to her request to return to Lincolnshire immediately to inform her family.

The only thing he had been unbending about was that she must return tonight. Then he had summoned one of the most beautiful carriages she had ever seen, and unceremoniously loaded her in it, uttering those compelling parting words. Anticipation? Or a warning…?

She forced her thoughts from her new husband, and let her plans for restoring Stonehaven occupy her mind. Only a skeleton staff operated the estate and had done so for years. She relished filling it with the full staff that was sorely needed. Her father had faced the looming threat of debtor prison, but no more. Joyous relief pulsed through her once more, overshadowing the worry that she must soon return to Sherring Cross.

The chaise rumbled into Stonehaven's courtyard, and she flew out the door as Flemings, the manor's sole footman, opened it for her. "Welcome back, Lady Jocelyn."

She smiled warmly at Flemings then hurried inside the massive oak door already held open by their butler, Cromwell.

"Welcome back, milady." He took her coat and smiled back — a rare thing. Her happiness must have been contagious.

"Where is my father, Cromwell? I am most anxious to speak with him."

"He is anxious to speak with ye as well, milady. He has been awaitin' your return in the green parlor."

Her steps faltered when she saw Cromwell's wrinkled forehead. His brown, rheumy eyes gazed at her with concern.

Oh, dear. "My father knows of my journey to Norfolk?" she asked.

"I believe so, milady."

"I see. Have Mrs. Winthrop bring tea and cake."

"Yes, milady."

She smiled tightly and hurried to the parlor. She blew into the room and saw her father, Archibald Grayson Rathbourne, the seventh Earl of Waverham staring out the window pensively at the east gardens, gardens that her mother had tended so lovingly. It was why Jocelyn had ensured they always had a gardener to maintain the exquisitely designed grounds that her mother had poured so much loving energy into, and to furnish her grave with fresh flowers at all times.

Her father was a portly man, more scholarly than physical. His hair had just begun to pepper with gray, and glasses were perched on his aquiline nose. He rose at her entrance and his eyes, so much like her own, lost their worried expression

"You're back, my dear! Now tell me where have you been since yesterday? I was concerned when you didn't appear for breakfast, and have been gone all these long hours. I received your note that you would spend the night with Cousin Rosamund, but it all sounded so mysterious and unexpected."

"Oh, Father." She rushed over and threw herself into his arms, hugging him tightly.

"You are trembling, Jocelyn."

She did not lift her face from the crook of his neck as the door opened. She listened to the footfalls of Mrs. Winthrop and the *clanks* of the china as she laid out the tea and cakes.

"Come, come. Let us sit down."

He led her to the sofa that was in desperate need of upholstery, its green color faded and discolored. She gratefully sank into its depth and smiled tenderly at the sight of her father pouring her tea and arranging her favorite sweet cakes on a plate. It bespoke how worried he must have been. She gratefully accepted the teacup, curling her hands around it, loving the warmth that flowed into her.

The sofa creaked as he sat. "Now tell me, my dear, what

has happened to put such a strange glint in your eyes?"

Jocelyn did not hesitate. The words tumbled from her lips, unstoppable as she poured out the day's events to her father. She paused several times to compose herself, and at last she met his gaze as she ended her tale. Her father's expression could only be described as flummoxed.

"Are you saying, my dear child, that you are now the Duchess of Calydon?"

"Yes, Father."

He stared at her in disbelief. "You are married to the Duke of Calydon, Sebastian Jackson Thornton?"

"Yes, Father!"

She fidgeted under his intense scrutiny.

Then his shoulders slumped. "My God. I have failed you."

With a gasp of distress, she leapt to sit beside him and clasped his hands. "You have not failed me, Father. Please do not say such a thing."

"You are obviously unaware of the reputation of the Duke of Calydon. He is very powerful, and Sherring Cross is one of the richest estates in the realm. But there were rumors that circulated about him years ago. Rumors of stunning depravity, of a duel, and of him killing his mistress."

Jocelyn recoiled in shock, withdrawing her hands from his. "What utter rubbish! The duke has never been embroiled in a scandal. Even so removed in the country, we would have heard about it."

She surged to her feet with sudden restless energy. She stalked to the windows and stared down at the flowers dotted with fine flakes of snow, trying to find some comfort from the uncertainty that flooded through her. She did not turn as he draped his hands over her shoulders.

"Think, my dear. He did not marry you because you waved a derringer at him. We're talking about the powerful Duke of Calydon, with direct familial connection to the prince regent. He is known to me, even here. If he hadn't wanted to wed, he wouldn't have done so."

"But—"

He squeezed her shoulders. "I say I have failed you because of my unwise investments and choices. I am ashamed because you felt you had to lie and deceive in order to wed. You are only twenty-one. You could still have had a season. With your charm and beauty, you would have received many offers. My foolish ways denied you the opportunity every young girl of society should have."

She twisted to face him. "No, Father. I have no regrets over something I have never experienced. There is more to life than balls and soirees, and I have attended many here in the country and in Devonshire."

He gave a wan smile. "Hardly the same thing."

She placed a finger on his lips, silencing him. "As Duchess of Calydon—" She inhaled as the words resounded in her. She continued shakily, "As the duchess, I will have many opportunities to take London and the glittering throng by storm, as you would say. I did not start out my rash scheme to entrap the duke, but Lord Anthony. Never did I imagine that Anthony would already be married, nor that the duke would respond favorably to my impetuous demand."

He gently brushed a stray lock of her hair that fell forward, and tucked it behind her ear. "But how could he resist such a catch?"

She gave a soft laugh. "I must admit that I, too, am at a loss as to why he wed me. I felt the entire time that he was the one in control and he was directing me toward his own agenda. But that could not be. We had never met until I entered his library."

"Perhaps Lord Anthony spoke about you?"

"I doubt it. I now realize that the few weeks Anthony spent here in Lincolnshire was merely to gain perspective on

Miss Peppiwell. There was a problem he often talked about, one that clouded his eyes with doubt. It must have been her."

"Were you hurt by Lord Anthony's defection?"

She considered. "No I am not. I had a grand time with him. He was witty and charming, and he danced beautifully. He did kiss me a few times, too, which was nice."

"Jocelyn!"

She laughed at the indignation on his face. "I now know they were very chaste kisses, Papa. But I was not so much angry that he made promises then broke them, as I was in despair. Because I had hung all my hopes for my family on marrying him. Not because I loved him."

"How do you know they were chaste kisses, Jocelyn?" The frost in his voice did not escape her. Heat blossomed in her cheeks, and she turned away.

Too late. He scowled as embarrassment swept through her. "Jocelyn?"

"Calydon— He kissed me. More than once."

Her father's jaw worked. "And you did not think *they* were chaste?"

She cleared her throat. "No, Father."

Something swept through his gray eyes that she could not decipher. "Did he kiss you before or after the wedding?"

"Before and after."

"Ah."

She did not understand his soft chuckle. "What, Papa?"

"Did you enjoy his attentions, child?"

"Father!" Her eyes widened. She swallowed as he patiently waited for her response. "I— I have never felt anything like it. Not even while racing Wind Dancer or dancing a waltz. I burned, yet I felt so alive," she whispered.

This time it was his eyes that widened, then he fussed with his tea cup. "You are deplorably honest, my dear. I pray you are not quite as guileless with the duke." He straightened and met her eyes. "You will, however, make him an excellent duchess. Your mother, bless her heart, ensured that you possess all the social grace and polish to walk beside him. I have no doubts you will succeed brilliantly at your new station in life."

Jocelyn smiled at her father. Thank goodness he did not condemn her for her actions. Her heart beat with enough trepidation already—that the duke would hold her in contempt after their wedding night. After all, if she had been seduced as she'd sworn, the matter of her virginity should not be a problem anymore. She wondered if he would be able to tell. She frowned thoughtfully. Could men tell? They must be able to. It would be foolhardy for the men of society to value a thing so greatly, and have no way of proving if the value is still intact. She could not ask her father, she was already mortified by discussing a simple kiss with him.

"I worry for you, my dear. I do not believe the duke is a man to trifle with. He has the power to crush you if you are not careful. His reputation may just be a rumor…it has been years since I've heard him spoken of, other than regarding his miraculous touch with investments."

"What have you heard, father? Back when the scandal happened." At his hesitation, she implored, "I return to him tonight. Please do not let me go in doubt."

After the deepest of sighs, he answered, "Rumors circulated of a duel, of a mistress that he strangled with his bare hands, and of the duke himself being murdered. The fact that he is clearly still alive could well mean they were all just foul rumors."

The room spun around her as a sick feeling roiled in her stomach. "Oh."

"It is an uncertain future that you have bound yourself to, my child," he said, his gaze filled with concern. "Just be careful."

"I will." She eased out the breath that had backed up

in her lungs. "To know that Victoria, Emily, and Emma will all have seasons and dowries, that Stonehaven will be made solvent for William..." Her smile wobbled as her father tenderly cupped her cheeks with his hands.

"You take too much upon yourself."

"Oh, Papa, to know that my little loves and you will now be safe and happy, that all makes it much more palatable to have married a man who may or may not have been involved in murder." She gripped his hands so fiercely that her father laughed, pulled her close, and hugged her tightly.

"My sweet child."

"What's done is done. You mustn't worry. I will not let rumors of the past affect me, and I will resolve to be as happy as I can be with my new husband."

A sharp pang went through her heart. She could only hope the man she married would feel the same about her when he learned the truth.

Chapter Four

Snow crunched beneath Jocelyn's boot heels as she alighted from the chaise.

Only a few lamps were lit in the courtyard, and they barely pierced the gray fog that blanketed the night. She almost stumbled at the line of servants that had assembled on the steps to greet her. The wind howled, and even through her winter coat, the cold bit at her bones. She shivered and pulled the cloak tighter, warding off the icy chill. She knew it was customary for the servants to be introduced to their new mistress, now the lady of the house, but she thought it unnecessary that they were lined up in the cold waiting for her.

Calydon appeared like a specter from the mist and stalked toward her. Images of a murdered mistress floated suddenly in her mind, and she tried to banish her dark thoughts. Without success.

A strange kind of dread gripped her, and she was barely aware when he introduced her to his staff as his new duchess. Her smile was wooden, and she went through the motions with a loud thundering in her head. It was only when she was swept through the massive hall that she realized it was her heartbeat pounding in her ears.

"Have you dined?" Sebastian asked politely.

She jumped, betraying her nervousness. "I did, Your Grace."

"Ah."

She felt compelled to fill the silence that pressed on so ominously. "I am sorry I'm a bit late in arriving...home. I needed to spend some time with my family preparing them for my sudden absence. My sisters are quite attached to me, even though I must admit they vibrated with excitement over the happy circumstances."

His only response was a grunt.

Her knees weakened as they started to climb the winding staircase. She glanced wildly behind her, but nary a servant was in sight. Did he mean to escort her straight to the bedding chamber? It was impossible to slow her racing heart. She was not sure what emotion filled her most at the thought of being ravished—dread or curiosity.

I am looking forward to our wedding night.

Since she hoped that meant he was prepared to enjoy it, she decided on curiosity.

She would not believe a gentleman would lead her straight to the event after travelling for hours in the chaise. Not without time to ready herself.

But then, he was not a gentleman, as proclaimed by his own words.

She was nervous, even though she had nearly convinced herself there was nothing to be afraid about.

Nearly.

She gulped as heat rushed through her at the memory of her father's talk. He had tried to tell her what to expect. She had been amazed, then stupefied as he had taken a seat before her, his complexion florid, and wheezing like a bellows. She had thought he was on the verge of a heart attack. Unfortunately, the only words he managed to utter did not reveal much about the act itself.

"Be brave," he'd said. "Be brave."

Then Mrs. Winthrop had not helped at all by telling her that she must not gainsay her husband, even if he wanted to do wicked and immoral things to her. Jocelyn could not imagine what could go on in a bed chamber that was wicked and immoral. She had rolled her eyes and said as much.

Mrs. Winthrop had then warned her in the most ominous voice, "Beware the devil's trap, girl."

She hadn't known that Mrs. Winthrop had it in her to be so dark and gloomy.

She and Sebastian reached the landing without him speaking. He seemed lost in thought…possibly plotting the wicked and immoral things he would do to her. The idea sent an unbidden curl of excitement through her body.

He stopped at a massive oak door carved with an intricate design of a dragon. "Your lady's maid will be here shortly to assist you."

Without another word he spun around to leave.

"Wait!"

"Yes, Jocelyn?"

"Will you…um— Will we…?"

The sensual smile that creased his handsome face was her answer.

She inhaled shakily, wrenched open the door, and stumbled hastily into the room.

Immediately, her gaze zeroed in on the bed. Good lord. She had never seen a bed so massive. Fashioned of the finest exotic woods, it was raised on a dais, and surrounded by dark blue and silver drapes hung from a high wooden frame and gathered at the corners with silver cords.

She blinked as she studied the room. The sheer size of it was boggling, but the design exquisite. Persian carpets covered the floor and all the furniture was oak with the strange dragon motif emblazoned on them. The colors of the decor, from the carpet, the billowing drapes, and sofas, were shades of deep blue with silver. The elegance of the room awed her.

But— Surely this was not her chamber. She walked over to the bed and flushed at the garment splayed in its center. She lifted the pale blue chiffon peignoir and swallowed at its sheerness. She dropped it and stepped away from the bed.

She spun as the door opened and a maid swept in with a curtsy. "Yer Grace, I am Rose, your lady's maid."

"Hello Rose." She smiled warmly, and started to unpin her hair as Rose hurried over to start unpacking her valise, which had somehow appeared.

"Would ye like a bath, Yer Grace?"

She gave her a tired nod, and sank into one of the sofas in the room. A moan slipped from her lips at the wonderful feel of the deep, soft cushions. Rose bustled with a jaunty kind of efficiency, disappearing several times into the adjoining room to prepare her bath.

"Are all the rooms this large, Rose?" Jocelyn called.

"No, Yer Grace, Mrs. Dudley says His Grace had this room specially designed."

"Oh? Is the duke's room just as large?"

She paused in rubbing the tightness from her neck at the bird-like look of inquiry that Rose threw her way.

"This is His Grace's room, Yer Grace."

Jocelyn surged to her feet, nervously searching the walls around her. "I do not see a connecting door to my own chamber."

"There is no duchess's chamber, Yer Grace."

"I beg your pardon?" The look on Jocelyn's face must have betrayed her shock.

Rose rushed to explain. "Mrs. Dudley says on account o' His Grace's parents' cold marriage with lots o' closed doors, he tore down the wall separatin' the duchess chambers from this one, so they made one big room. Mrs. Dudley says it must be on account o' the duke not wantin' such a cold marriage."

Trepidation surged through Jocelyn at this bit of information. "I see." She remained quiet as Rose undressed her and led her to the bath chamber. "Oh, my!"

"It's a beauty ain't it? His Grace had it fixed up with the latest modern plumbin' a few years ago."

Jocelyn hastily stripped off her dressing gown, stepped into the marble Grecian bathtub, and sank into the welcome heat of the water. She rubbed the scented jasmine soap over her arms, neck, and chest, her mind swirling with the idea that Sebastian did not want a cold marriage with separate chambers from his wife. Still, it was never prudent to listen to servants' gossip. For all she knew, he'd removed the walls and connecting door for some completely unrelated reason.

She sank deep into the tub, all but purring in enjoyment as the heat of the water soothed the tenseness from her body, and she savored the luxurious bath to its fullest.

She refused to dwell with fear on the coming night, when her new husband would return to the chamber…to do wicked and immoral things to her.

• • •

He'd acquired a duchess.

Standing at the open library window, Sebastian dipped his hand in his trouser pocket, touching the locket that Anthony had given her. A wry smile twisted his lips and he raised his glass in a mock toast to his mother and drank.

His mother had given Sebastian the locket several years ago, telling him to bequeath it to his duchess for a future daughter, as it had belonged to the first born females in her family for several generations. As turned off by the notion of marriage as he was, he had gifted it to a reluctant Anthony for his first born daughter, instead.

When the locket had clattered across his desk to him, Sebastian had been stunned to realize the feeling that powered through him at the sight of it was relief. The necklace was back in his possession. It had never occurred that the heirloom meant so much to him.

He had sworn never to marry, comfortable to pass his several entailments to Anthony, even though Sebastian knew that wasn't a burden his brother wanted. Anthony wanted to live free, sail the oceans, and visit the Americas and the Caribbean with his Miss Peppiwell. He continually expounded to Sebastian that he wanted to be unencumbered, to live his life as he wished, not be shackled to a handful of family piles containing only bad memories.

Unfortunately, Sebastian shared the sentiment.

The clock in the library chimed, signaling the midnight hour. He wondered if Jocelyn had fallen into slumber. He had secluded himself in the room where he felt most comfortable, to give her time to prepare, and had become lost in his thoughts for at least an hour. Was she waiting on him with virginal anxiety clothed in the provocative peignoir he'd had his lawyer acquire for him in London? Or had she fallen asleep, too exhausted from the day's events to care about her wedding night?

His mouth curled in disdain.

A virgin.

He took a healthy swallow of the whisky that burned all the way down, filling him with the warmth that was desperately needed in the library. He stood with the tall windows open, the chilly air whistling in, deep and biting. He could never understand why he liked the cold so much. The fireplace that roared behind him did little to dull the ache that filled his bones, its only purpose to shed light into the room. The wind howled, and flecks of snow blew in, stinging his face and neck.

Jocelyn had lied about Anthony seducing her. Sebastian detested liars. He took some comfort from the fact that she was completely transparent with her emotions. Indeed, he did not doubt that Anthony had teased and flirted with her, and even made promises of marriage. The necklace being in her possession showed that his brother had, at least momentarily, questioned the depth of his affections for Miss Peppiwell. But he had not bedded Jocelyn.

He might well have gone far enough for her to be deemed wholly compromised by society. But clearly, he had not even kissed her properly.

Sebastian muttered a curse as his cock came to life, and his grip on the whiskey glass tightened at the memory of the taste of her lips and her passionate response.

He understood Anthony's slight defection from Miss Peppiwell. Jocelyn's dark beauty was astonishing. Her skin was smooth and flawless, though her cheeks had been kissed by the sun, showing him she spent a lot of time outdoors. Her luxurious mane of raven hair with her storm-cloud eyes had a stunning effect on his senses. Yet, it was not her beauty that intrigued him. There were too many beauties in London, eager to been seen with him at balls and operas and desperate to be in his bed, for him to be enchanted by appearance. Beauty alone had never piqued his interest.

Jocelyn fascinated him. It was her fiery temperament that drew him most. He already knew she wasn't a simpering fool. He had no time for the vain and frivolous women of society. He viewed the sweet-tempered, pliable young misses straight from the schoolroom with disdain. None would dare storm his estate and point a derringer at him, a duke, demanding the stain on her honor be satisfied.

The *ton* would be titillated to know that was how the arrogant Duke of Calydon had wed. The scandal would roar like an unquenchable fire.

Distaste curled his stomach at the fickleness of society. The scandal would die under the onslaught of his undeniable power. For he controlled the purse strings of many families through his investments. Days later, they would all simper to be seen with her, and be invited to the balls she would come to host. She would probably be declared "an original" for how she had snared him, where a less fortunate woman would be an outcast for life.

He pulled the locket from his pocket and held it up in the glow of the fire and moonlight, despising the relief he felt to have back what she'd gifted to him.

His father had died in a carriage accident several years past, and his mother, Margaret Abigail Jackson, the dowager Duchess of Calydon, had not even honored the appropriate mourning period before wedding her lifelong lover. She had not suffered the condemnation of society overly much, either.

Her eldest son, on the other hand, had long harbored a fathomless disdain for her because of her illicit affair and complete disregard for his father. A contempt so deep Sebastian had hardly deigned to speak with her. After he came into the title, he had wasted no time in banishing her to the dowager house and cutting off her allowance, ignoring her pleas, cold and indifferent to the perfidious female's tears and machinations.

A few months back the family solicitor had hand-delivered her secret cache of diaries, written over the years of his childhood. His father had held them in his possession and left instruction for them to be handed to Sebastian at a certain time. He glanced at the packet of bound journals on his desk still awaiting him to read them fully. His parents had endured a cold marriage, never kissing or touching. He barely remembered any words or gestures of affection at all, only the perfunctory kiss his father normally placed on her forehead, unable to do more in the face of her revulsion for him. Sebastian had hated her after discovering her in the garden with her lover at the tender age of six, furious at realizing the cause of the constant arguments which had resulted in the nearly total absence of his father from his life.

All because she had a lover whom she could not relinquish.

Two things he learned from the couple of diaries he'd read thus far: his unfaithful bitch of a mother loved her paramour unashamedly and unreservedly, and she'd abhorred the touch of his father, who worshipped the ground she walked on. Sebastian had suspected what he would find, but had still found it difficult to read the words of a woman he had once loved. She had hardly found it fit to love him in return, too busy with her lover. The pain he felt reading her words had been too real, so he had yet to read the remainder.

Her journals also brought home another inescapable fact. That he needed an heir. His father had not been lying in the letters he left for him. When he wrote about Anthony not being his son, Sebastian had thought it bitter ranting. However, her diaries revealed Anthony and Constance to be the children of her lover. His father had proof of this as he had not been in her bed for years, and he also had one of her journal as irrevocable evidence. His father hated his wife's perfidy so much that he had promised to use the journal to renounce Anthony and Constance, if Sebastian did not marry and obtain an heir for himself.

Sebastian had told Anthony, and let him read the damning letter his father left him. The pain that had flared in his brother's eyes had punched Sebastian deep. He had seen right through the laughter and quip that Anthony now understood why their father had always been so cold with him.

Sebastian had promised to fight the provisions their father had implemented with the lawyer. But Anthony had refused, fearing how scandal would devastate their sister and mother. And it was possible that even now Anthony's nemesis was hinting of his illegitimacy, and the rumors were being whispered, already tainting Constance, diminishing her chances of marrying well. Sebastian had seen the profound relief in his brother at being freed of the unwanted responsibility of their father's titles. So he knew he had no choice in the matter.

He could not bear the idea of his titles and lands passing to strangers, or worse, reverting to the crown. The estates, the tenants, the responsibilities of nobility that he had learned at his father's knee, the things that had bound them together in respect and a common purpose from the day he was born, were his to shoulder, and his alone.

Except—

Marriage had always left a sour taste in his mouth, and until the fateful day he had learned otherwise, he had always believed women served but one purpose.

But then, at thirty, he found himself suddenly resolved to the idea of a wife. He had duly composed a list of eligible females. The chore had left the most God-awful taste in his mouth. And just as he'd been about to resign himself to the worst fate imaginable, something miraculous had happened.

Jocelyn had crashed into his life pointing a gun right at his jaded heart.

Disbelief and fascination had held him immobile in his chair as she had pointed the laughable weapon at him. He could have easily relieved her of it anytime he wished, but he had been too riveted by the drama unfolding before his eyes.

He'd known in an instant he had to possess her.

And so, in the space of one brief meeting, he found himself a married man, with his tempting duchess awaiting him in their chambers. A wife who would brighten his life, and share his burdens. He knew it was all right there for him to reach out and take.

But he also knew he could never relent and trust his wife completely.

Chapter Five

Jocelyn's slender, graceful back was turned to Sebastian, and he could see the fine tremors that sifted along her frame at his entrance.

He closed the door with a soft *snick,* but she did not turn to face him from where she stood in front of the windows gazing into the bright starlit night.

He had thought she might be hiding under the covers, or at least pretending to be asleep. A pleased smile curved his lips as he observed her. He should have known she would confront things head on, despite her fears. Hadn't she done that very thing this morning?

He did not have to wait long for the familiar rush of desire that hardened his cock. He paused in removing his dinner jacket, startled by how visceral the need to hold her was. She still did not stir. She had no clue that he was removing every stitch of his clothes. Or perhaps she did. With every rustle and noise he made undressing, her frame tensed and shook with even more tremors. Her hands, held at her sides, clasped and unclasped, moved to form a tight ball at her front.

Suddenly she spun around to face him, her glorious mane of hair that had been loosely pinned tumbling to her back and shoulders. He met her eyes and a shock of surprise pulsed through him.

His intrepid duchess was not trembling from nervousness or anxiety, after all. The storm clouds that had gathered in her eyes, threatening to break any second, were tempestuous ones. He expected to see a flash of lightening and hear the crash of thunder any moment now.

His beautiful duchess was enraged.

He smiled with satisfaction, and his cock swelled in anticipation.

This…should prove interesting.

• • •

Jocelyn's rage was so intense she felt like a bowstring drawn to the verge of snapping.

"Do you realize you've had me waiting for almost two hours? With no consideration for the uncertainty I may be feeling?"

His head tilted insolently. "Have I?"

Her rage burned brighter at the complete lack of remorse reflected in his wintry blues.

She had been pampered and scented, her hair brushed for what felt like a thousand strokes, and then dressed in the peignoir he had gifted her. It was so sheer her heart still palpitated at the thought. All for his bloody pleasure. And the conceited cad had kept her waiting. Two miserable hours.

"Why, you conceited bas—"

The rest of the words strangled in her throat as he dropped the garment he had been holding loosely in front of him.

In a shocked daze, her eyes tracked its fall to the carpet and scanned the pieces of clothing strewn about haphazardly—his jacket, waistcoat, his pants, boots, and assorted unmentionables.

She gasped and snapped her head up, and her eyes popped as she beheld her husband standing there.

Gloriously naked.

My God. He was splendid.

She drank in the sight of him, from his slashing brows to his chiseled jaw and sensual lips, down his powerful body. He was tall and sleek with a broad chest, wide, athletic shoulders, and thighs and calves that were hard with muscle. Everything about him was hard, strong, and proud. She had never imagined the male body could be so…beautiful.

Her hands fluttered to her throat as she stared at the part of him that jutted out toward her, so hard and rigid. And huge.

Good heavens.

She snapped her gaze up and met his eyes. They smoldered with something primitive and predatory that took her breath away.

In two strides he was directly in front of her. Then he reached out, hauled her into his arms. And he took.

His fingers locked into the thick coils of her hair as he angled his head and crushed his lips over hers. He was not slow and seductive as he'd been earlier, instead he devoured. The intensity of his kiss shook her enough that fear once again slammed through her stuttering her heart.

She gasped into his mouth, and his tongue plundered, entwining with hers, lashing her with unexpected pleasure. She moaned as that same unfamiliar fire swept through her body. A strange buzzing whipped through her and she whimpered as he pressed her back into the icy cold wall. Need pulsed between her legs, melting her and creating sensations there that left her weak and stunned.

She felt as if everything was happening too fast. A sharp rip sounded, and her sheer nightgown parted down the middle. She let out a yelp as he hoisted her, and she instinctively wrapped her legs around his waist. She felt hot and restless, her skin painfully sensitive. His hands moved over her, caressing her buttocks, then cupping her breasts. He dragged his thumb across her nipple, and the rough caress slammed pleasure directly to her core. His kisses and nips stroked over her lips, her throat, her collar bone, and she arched in a stinging ache of pleasure as his mouth clamped over her nipple and sucked. She gripped his dark head tight as he pulled strongly with his mouth, destroying her with the electric sensations he sent flooding through her entire body.

The hand not pinning her to the wall sent flames of heat streaking up her thighs and between her legs. Shock and excitement vied for equal attention when he parted her curls and ran his fingers though her slit. She was mortifyingly wet there, and she desperately wondered if she should be. Her thoughts derailed as he plunged a long finger inside her while circling his thumb just above, touching a knot of agonizing pleasure.

She splintered.

Her scream was muffled as he captured her lips, kissing her in time to the fingers that continued to torment her between her legs. She felt delirious with the unbearably hot desires twisting within her. She shook with the pleasure, the lightening that struck her, and the fever that invaded her limbs, too wrapped in the overwhelming physical sensations to care about the liquid that wetted his hands and slickness that ran between her thighs.

He plunged a second finger inside, and she cried out at the bite of pain. He did not give her time to adjust to the invasion before he continued thrusting. Sweat slicked her skin and she was dazedly grateful, for it seemed to cool the fire that burned so hotly in her veins. The room spun as he tumbled her down on the bed.

His lips left hers and created a wake of scalding heat as he licked down to her breasts, dipped in her navel, and continued down.

Shocked embarrassment stormed through her as he replaced his wet fingers with his mouth and tongue. She shrieked, her back bowing under the riotous sensations that gripped her. His tongue speared inside her and fiery tingles coursed through her body. She gripped a fistful of his hair and yanked. She was surprised when he came up easily, his muscled framed poised over hers as he stared down at her, his eyes glittering with heat.

She gasped raggedly and stared back at him with her heart jerking and thundering painfully.

She could not stop the tremors that shook her, try as she might.

"Ah, Jocelyn." The softest of kisses brushed her swollen lips. "I have not lost so much control since I was an untried boy." His lips gentled even further as he kissed her cheeks, her eyelids, and back to softly fluttering over her lips.

Instead of his hands burning her with pleasure, they now ran languidly over her, gentle and teasing, but with a focused intensity that wrung soft moans and gasps from her. The sharp, desperate edgy feeling eased, replaced by languorous pleasure.

"It surely must be wicked and immoral to feel so good," she moaned against his lips, her focus blurring at the feel of his skin rubbing sensually against hers.

He chuckled softly. "We haven't even begun to be wicked and immoral yet, my duchess."

The edgy uncertainty and fear she had felt earlier fled completely, and a tentative trust formed, allowing her to relax into the pleasure he bestowed upon her body. She trusted him wholly when he eased her over so that she lay on her stomach, and she could only purr deep in her throat as he kissed and nibbled her neck, over her shoulder blades, and down her back, stopping at her buttocks. He nipped sharply. Her hips rolled and arched up, loving the heat of his tongue as it soothed the sting. She purred, squirming under his sensual touch. His chuckle vibrated against her, and his crooning words of encouragement as he licked a sensitive spot behind her knees had almost as strong an effect as the fingers that continued to thrust so steadily inside her.

She shivered, moaning weakly, helplessly craving the pleasure he tormented her with. His powerful hands gripped her hips and spun her to face him. She swallowed at the dark sensuality that marked his features. Without breaking their gazes, he drew her under him, lifting her legs to hook at his hips.

She ran her hands over his arms and chest, reveling in his strength and power. Her hands drifted down his roped abdomen, then hesitated.

His breath fanned over her lips as he exhaled. "Touch me, my duchess. Do not shy away now."

He gritted his teeth and groaned as she circled his hard length with her fingers. He felt like hot iron.

"*Sebastian*." Her moan was an entreaty to fill the emptiness that clawed at her.

He growled in answer.

His movements were rough when he parted her thighs and started to push into her. His lips captured hers, claiming her tongue in a teasing foray as he slowly thrust, deeper and deeper. A burning pleasure-pain consumed her, bowing her back, and had her bucking and moaning in his mouth. He held himself taut above her, his body shaking as he waited for her to adjust.

She felt stretched, wonderfully full, and excited by what was happening. An excitement that tunneled into amazed wonder at the sensations that gripped her as he started a powerful lunge and retreat.

The sharp pain had been fleeting, and now the sweetest pleasure she had ever felt spiraled from her center and ignited within her. Her hips instinctively arched, undulating to the rhythm of his powerful thrusts. She could not contain her moans or the strength with which she clutched him as sensual pleasure held her in a vise. She wrapped her legs higher around his waist and was rewarded as he plunged deeper. She screamed as the pleasure roared through her, fierce and sweet, and she exploded in a conflagration of delight. Sebastian's harsh groan rumbled against her lips as he kissed her, plunging with increased power and speed until the pleasure overtook him, too.

"Bloody hell," she whispered against his lips long moments later, her frame still trembling from the mind-numbing pleasure.

"I should have known that cursing was part of your repertoire," he mumbled with a chuckle.

He rolled with her so that she splayed on top of him. She reared up to look at him, searching his face. She followed the scar that ran from his temple and across his cheeks so savagely. Instead of giving him a grisly mien, it hinted at rakish danger. She smiled at her thoughts.

"Not many see my scar and smile, Duchess." His voice was still husky from their lovemaking, and an answering thrill surged through her.

"I like it." When his eyes shuttered, she lowered her face so less than an inch separated their lips, and asked, "Disappointed? Did you expect me to scream or cry?"

A warning growl rumbled from his chest. "I have had young ladies faint at the sight of my visage, Duchess."

"I find you devastatingly handsome, and I simply don't believe anyone fainted from this little scratch." She brushed her lips across his scar, trailing soft kisses over the crescent shape. She halted her movements when she realized how still he had become. The hands that had been loosely wrapped around her waist had tightened painfully. But she did not protest. She raised up, observing his expressionless face. "What?"

"Being hidden away from society, you obviously have not had a chance to look upon many handsome faces to judge accurately, Duchess."

Even though said with a smile playing at his lips, she had a feeling he was not amused. The curve of his mouth held no warmth, and she could glean nothing from his cool gaze.

"I disagree," she said quietly.

Suddenly she wished for the privacy of her own chambers, unsure how to deal with her husband's changeable moods. Especially while splayed over him, naked. Heat rushed through her and her discomfort grew.

"You're blushing, Duchess. I believe I would give you one of my finest studs for your thoughts right now."

"Indeed?" She raised skeptical brows. "Many would only offer a penny."

"I did not think a penny would entice you to reveal the unladylike thoughts that have you blushing so becomingly and averting your eyes from mine."

She smiled hesitantly, heating even more. "In truth, I was thinking of all the wicked and immoral things we just did."

Laughter burst from him. "Ah, Duchess, you have much to learn. We have done nothing wicked or immoral. Yet," he added with a sinful smile.

She sucked in a breath. "Show me." The words came out as more of a moan than the demand she had meant it to be.

His hands had cupped the curve of her backside and one slipped lower, his fingers teasing her wetness. "My pleasure, my incorrigible duchess. My pleasure."

. . .

The early fog that rolled in through the windows Sebastian had opened sometime during the night obscured the soft rays of the rising sun.

He shifted in the bed, the unfamiliar feel of a female body curved so trustingly into his side startling him for a moment. He had bedded many women, but never had he slept through the night with one. Not even Marissa, his only mistress, as she had belonged to another.

His gut tightened as he recalled the many ways Jocelyn had surrendered to him, over and over through the night. She made love as she did everything else, with boldness and fire. If he had not breached her maidenhead himself, he probably would have doubted her innocence. After the first wave of loving, her unguarded responses had almost bewitched him. She was a fast pupil, and at one point he had felt as though he was the student and she the teacher as she licked and caressed him with a natural sensuality that had drowned him in sensations he had never felt before.

A derisive smile curved his lips and he grunted softy. A simple memory of her hot mouth over his cock had him forgetting how perfidious women were. He must take care with this woman. She could so easily make him want to let down his guard.

He gently eased her head from his shoulder, moving silently to stand before the windows. He drew open the drapes that were only slightly parted. The fog rolled over the hills, casting gray shadows over the land. A soft moan came from the bed and he turned to observe her. She wriggled, murmuring in her sleep. His gut clenched when his name whispered from her lips on a loving sigh, then she settled into deeper slumber.

He was annoyed that he wanted to join her. Instead,

he forced himself to turn away, and opened the door to his dressing room. He could not admit his valet to dress him — not with his duchess splayed so wantonly on the sheets. He had not given a thought to how tearing down the walls that separated the two master chambers would affect the logistics of daily life. He only knew he'd wanted no closed doors between him and his future wife. His mother had used the connecting doors like an ice fortress his father had been unable to breach. He'd sworn he would never allow himself to be in such a situation if he were to ever marry. A locked bedchamber would not become a weapon between him and his duchess, ever. And if that meant dressing themselves, so be it. He wanted no other eyes but his on Jocelyn in her present state of undress.

He did not choose to analyze the feeling. He also ignored the yearning to return to the bed and wrap himself around her. He did not possess one of the biggest fortunes in England because he lay abed. He had much to do. His solicitor should be on his way with documents outlining the settlement that would be paid to her father, the sum that he would settle as dowries on his new sisters-in-law, accounts to be opened for Jocelyn at the milliners and modistes, and an amount set for her allowance.

There was no time for idle pleasures.

No matter how much he wanted to return to the unexpected warmth of his new bride's arms.

Chapter Six

When Jocelyn awoke, she was certain she was in love. The chill in the bedchamber could not daunt her spirits as she untangled her limbs from the linens. The massive drapes were drawn, and the sun poured its rays through the several windows. The panes were closed, but she saw that the fireplace had died to low embers, accounting for the chill in the air.

She felt the most glorious smile lift her lips along with her spirits. Sebastian had been magnificent. She could not fathom why her father told her to be brave, or why Mrs. Winthrop thought anything could be immoral.

But it was true, Jocelyn certainly felt wicked.

The feelings Sebastian roused in her were a surprise, to say the least, but she welcomed them. He was sinfully sensuous, and all hers.

She laughed as she jumped from the bed, ringing the bell for her lady's maid. She did not have to wait long for Rose, and she bathed and dressed with her assistance. Jocelyn did not want her hair pinned up, but instead she left it uncoiled, brushing against her hips with every sway. She dressed in her very finest yellow muslin morning dress. It was from last season, but it complemented her complexion and the dark luster of her hair.

Curious about the household, she went in search of her husband.

Within a few hours, Jocelyn was sure of two things.

First, she doubted that the glow she'd had when she awoke was love. The feeling had burned away too quickly in her disappointment and anger.

She breakfasted alone in the morning room, having learned that the duke had eaten much earlier and was now ensconced in his library dealing with business matters. She had been undaunted after being warned by the housekeeper, and had entered his private domain without invitation. He had been so cold and remote at her simple query as to how he fared that morning, that she had been completely flummoxed. He had summarily dismissed her, indicating the depth of work he had waiting, and that he would see her for supper.

Supper!

Where had the teasing lover of last night gone? She felt miffed, and more than a little hurt that he had not deigned to speak with her after the wonderful experiences they had shared on their wedding night. Their *wedding night*. If this was an indication of things to come, things were bound to get tumultuous, for she could not accept such coldness after their firestorm of passion.

She paused on the way to the parlor as a shocking thought occurred to her. What if feeling those incredible things was a common occurrence to the duke, nothing to be in awe and amazement over?

She banished the thought, hating the ugly jealousy that griped her at the mere notion. After a tour of the large, stately manor and speaking with Mrs. Otterbsy, the head housekeeper, Jocelyn realized that the estate ran with a grim efficiency that needed little to no input from her. Everything Mrs. Otterbsy presented to her had been in proper order, and she could find no fault.

The second thing Jocelyn realized was that she was completely and utterly bored. The concept so stunned her that for a few minutes she did not know what to do. She was always occupied at full tilt running Stonehaven, so to now be a duchess who sat on a luxurious cushion with her thumbs twiddling and nothing else to do—it would soon drive her mad.

When she could stand it no longer, she had launched into motion, ordering up the carriage.

She now stood in front of her old home.

The door flew open before she had a chance to ring the knocker. "Milady." Cromwell did not look surprised to see her.

She sailed inside, loving the feeling that swept through her as Emma and William spied her from the parlor. Their shrieks rang joyously in her ears as they tumbled into her arms.

"Come now," she said, laughing. "Have you turned into little barbarians after only a day?"

"I fear they have, Jocelyn."

She glanced up at the teasing reply of her sister, Victoria. Only a year separated them, and Victoria was her dearest friend. She could see the concern in her sister's eyes, and Jocelyn smiled at her in reassurance.

"Where is Papa? I will see him first, then visit with you," she said, shooing the twins.

Victoria went with her as they strolled toward the library. "Are you truly well?"

Jocelyn glanced up to see her searching her face with her expressive hazel eyes—eyes that reminded her so much of their mama. "Yes, I am truly well."

There was a slight pause and then her sister asked, "Were you brave?"

The surprised laughter that spilled from Jocelyn had Victoria laughing with her. "Oh, goodness, Vicki."

"You must tell me, sister dear." Victoria gulped. "Please do not fear for my delicate sensibilities. I must know what happened."

"Oh, I fear your sensibilities are in for a treat. It was glorious!"

"Was it wicked and immoral?" The question was spoken in a hushed whisper.

Their gales of laughter were cut short by her father opening the library door. He arched his bushy brows at her. "I see you have suffered no ill effects from your evening trek to Norfolk, my dear." Her father brushed his lips against her forehead in greeting.

"I will have Mrs. Winthrop bring tea and cake, Papa," Victoria said. "And I will tell Emily you are here, Jocelyn. She has been ensconced in the schoolroom all morning with some medieval text, completely enraptured." She hurried away, leaving Jocelyn alone with her father.

Jocelyn groaned as she sank into the library sofa. She turned toward her father, loving that he sat beside her instead of behind his desk.

"I had not expected you to visit so soon."

She let out a breath. "I was dreadfully bored, with little to do, Papa. The estate is run with frightening efficiency, and I fear I am at a loss with a day of complete leisure."

The corner of his eyes crinkled as he chuckled. "Your life will doubtless be much different. You must now host balls, soirees, and luncheons. And attend operas and masquerades with His Grace. You have been running this household for a very long time, my girl, ensuring all our needs are met. You must now do so for your own home, albeit in a different way.

Victoria and I will manage splendidly in your absence."

She sighed gustily. "I wanted to see Sebastian this morning, Papa, to discuss the renovation of Stonehaven. But when I left at noon he was *still* secluded in his library, working."

"No, no. That won't be necessary."

"Papa?"

"The Duke's solicitor paid me a visit this morning. It is all settled."

"Oh?"

She shifted to fully face her father. She barely glanced at Victoria when she came in with Mrs. Winthrop and the refreshments. Her father was silent as he waited for the housekeeper to serve them.

Jocelyn tapped her foot impatiently. "What do you mean his solicitor visited this morning?" she burst out after Mrs. Winthrop had departed. "Sebastian did not mention such a thing to me."

"Sit down, dear," he said to Victoria. "This interests you, as well."

Jocelyn bit her lip, glowering at her father. Then she sat stunned as her father told them the details of the solicitor's visit.

Well, she thought in astonishment when he was finished. It seemed she must have pleased her husband, after all.

· · ·

"Are you very disappointed that he did not share the financial settlements with you?"

Jocelyn glanced up from a bench in her mama's favorite garden. Its dark, luxurious beauty dotted with snow had done little to soothe her. She had visited with the twins and Emily, an occasion that had put her unease at bay for a while. But it had flared to life the minute she was alone. She had come outside to clear her head, feeling suffocated under the curious stares of her father and sister.

Her smile was strained. "Not really. I do feel odd that he wouldn't discuss something so important with me. But I realize I do not know him. He may not have thought it necessary to discuss it with me. I must remember we've only been wed for one day."

Victoria clasped her hand as she sat beside her. "Oh, Jocelyn, I could scarcely believe what Papa was saying. His Grace bestowed one hundred thousand pounds upon Papa for your hand! And Emily, Emma, and I are practically heiresses! Why do you think he provided dowries for us, or allowed Papa to partake in his latest investment scheme?"

Jocelyn was just as mystified. "I do not know. I had planned to speak with him today about restoring Stonehaven. We hardly had time for any discussions yesterday. Everything happened in such a whirlwind."

"Not even when you returned?"

"Especially then!" Jocelyn giggled at the scandalized gape that Victoria gave her. "I am so grateful to him. I came to him with no dowry but he made such generous settlements. Now I won't have to worry about any of you. And, Victoria, You can have a wonderful season! And I will be there as Duchess of Calydon to sponsor you into society."

"What will be the first event you will host, Jocelyn?" her sister asked, gripping Jocelyn's hands and practically vibrating with excitement.

"At first I thought of a winter ball. But I am unsure where to start planning a grand event like that. Then I realized that Christmas is only four weeks away. I would love for us all to be under one roof as a family. So, I've decided I will hold a family dinner."

Victoria squealed, clapping her hands with glee. "That would be wonderful, to dine at the magnificent Sherring Cross.

The twins and Emily will be so excited to have a magnificent Christmas dinner."

They looked wistfully around the gardens, sharing the same thought—a memory of their last Christmas dinner with their mother. They had never had another since, and it was something they had both always yearned for.

"Oh, Jocelyn," Victoria breathed. "It will be a beautiful holiday."

"I believe it will be, sister." Jocelyn kept smiling through a twinge of unbidden foreboding. "I truly hope it will be."

• • •

Jocelyn arrived back at Sherring Cross in time for the evening meal. The journey home had taken a couple of hours, though it had seemed much shorter with the riot of thoughts that had consumed her the whole way home.

She dressed for dinner in her finest evening gown that had a low waist and bared the rounded slopes of her breasts. Rose had done up her hair in an intricate Grecian knot, saying it highlighted the graceful arch of Her Grace's neck.

Jocelyn was gratified to see the glitter in Sebastian's eyes as they sat down to dine. Pigeon soup, roasted duck in butter almond sauce, and wild rice with leeks was the first course.

They ate in silence for a few minutes before she spoke. "I visited my father today."

"Mrs. Otterbsy informed me of your journey." He arched a brow in question, and Jocelyn plowed ahead.

"He told me of the settlements you bestowed, and I wanted to thank you."

Sebastian waved it off. "It is my duty to see to my family's welfare."

She stared at him uneasily, and cut into the pigeon. She chewed slowly, watching him as he watched her. A tingle unfurled inside her. From the intensity of his stare, she knew exactly what he was thinking about. A blush heated her cheeks, and she reached for her glass of wine.

"Why did you not discuss with me your decisions?" she asked.

He lowered his fork and regarded her. "It did not concern you."

"Of course it did. It was about me and my family."

"I will make a note of that for future reference," he said coolly.

His tone rang of finality, and she glared at him, stabbing the pigeon with her fork.

"I have sent in an announcement to the papers that we are wed. You can expect droves of callers, and even more invitations. Accept or reject them as you will. Oh, and a modiste from London will be visiting to outfit you with the latest fashions."

Her back went ramrod straight. "Indeed? I would appreciate that you at least include me in decisions that involve me directly, Sebastian."

"Do you object to the modiste's visit, or the announcement of our marriage?"

"No, of course not." she all but growled at him.

"Then I fail to understand your pique." He seemed genuinely puzzled.

The man was maddening! "It's what a married couple does," she said frostily. "They communicate, and learn to share, and make decisions together."

"I see." He lowered his fork completely. "You have been married before, to come by your knowledge?"

She took a sip of her wine, holding his gaze steadily. "No, I have not been married before. Nor have you. But I feel that to be happy and form a genuine attachment with mutual respect for one another, we must learn to speak openly. It is in the same spirit as your belief that we should have no closed doors between our bedchambers."

The smile that formed on his lips could have been one of admiration, but she was not completely sure.

"I concede, then. I will strive to be more open with you."

She cleared her throat. "And I *also* believe that we should endeavor to be in each other's company for at least one hour every day."

He leaned back in the elegantly carved dining chair. "I am confident you will expound on that with little prodding from me."

She inhaled deeply. "Our first night together was incredible." Heat suffused her face, but she refused to break eye contact. "It's something I will always remember. But then today, you shut yourself away from me without a word, even pushing me out when I came to say good morning. I found your behavior baffling and hurtful."

His jaw worked. "I see."

She feared if she stopped now she would never get it all out, and her marriage would be doomed, so she plunged on. "It will not do for us to ignore each other during the day, each busy with some task or other, then fall into pleasure at night. Our marriage would not be based on anything of real substance, don't you agree? I think an hour is not too much to ask of you."

His gaze was completely shuttered by the time she finished. The seconds stretched out so long in such total silence that she worried she had made a dreadful mistake.

Her breath eased out in relief when he lifted his wineglass to her with a smile on his lips. "Come here Jocelyn."

He dismissed the footmen with a glance. She went over to him, slightly nervous. She squeaked when he pulled her into his lap.

"Sebastian." she whispered, scandalized.

He seared her lips with a kiss and she melted in his embrace.

"An hour a day," he conceded between hard presses of kiss. "Then in the night when you tumble into my arms you will burn. There are times when I will be rough, riding you hard and quick."

She moaned as he took her mouth in a drugging kiss.

Pleasure deepened his voice. "And then there will be the unhurried nights, when I take you slow and leisurely."

"Don't forget the days," she murmured against his lips.

His laugh rumbled through her. "The days will be sinful, too, Duchess."

A thrill skittered through her, terrifying and exhilarating. An overwhelming desire to make him need her as much as she feared she was beginning to burn for him swept through her. She sank into his kiss, her tongue loving his.

And she ignored the insidious little voice that whispered it was all a lie, and that she was leading her foolish heart straight to a wealth of pain.

Chapter Seven

"We do not celebrate Christmas in this family." Sebastian's tone was so forbidding that Jocelyn hesitated to speak further.

She rolled over on her side, taking in his magnificent form as he gazed out the window at the rolling planes of his estate.

"Why not?" she asked, her voice soft, her body sated. "The holiday season is magical. The laughter, the gathering of families and friends, and the gifts. It's a beautiful time to grow closer, Sebastian. My sisters and I have longed for such a gathering, the last one we experienced was before our mother's passing. The twins have never enjoyed such a festive occasion," she said wistfully.

She waited patiently for his reply, too boneless to join him by the windows. The past two weeks had passed in stunning pleasure. Especially their nights. But in fact, the days held nearly the same enthrallment.

The hour each day that she had demanded had gradually lengthened to two hours, then three, which they spent either on a picnic, visiting his tenants, fishing through the ice holes on his lakes, or racing horses. Even though she loved their outdoor activities, their evenings of seclusion in the library, where they played chess or read in companionable silence, were the hours she treasured most. The nights left her weak and craving, filled with intense loving and passionate embraces. Those were the times she felt closest to him, and where he lost the reins of control that he held onto so tightly during the days.

In the night he was her lover in all ways—playful, gentle, demanding, fierce, and always intense. She fluffed several of the pillows and lazed her back against them. She furrowed her brows as she waited for him at least to acknowledge her wishes. His reaction had surprised her. Tonight was the first time she had mentioned the idea of a family gathering on Christmas to him. Victoria had visited several times, and they had been having tremendous fun organizing with Mrs. Otterbsy.

She saw the muscle in his jaw jump several times, a sure sign she had struck some kind of nerve with him.

"If you insist on having such a gathering," he ground out, "you will strike the Dowager Duchess from the guest list."

"Sebastian!" She scrambled from the bed, drawing on her silk robe to stand beside him. "She's your mother. Please explain."

He turned to her, and her heart lurched at his closed, hard face. She had not seen that shuttered expression in his eyes for more than a week. His guardedness had disappeared after the first week, and she had reveled in his relaxed manner. It made her think he might truly be happy with her.

"The subject is closed, Jocelyn. Anthony and the Peppiwells are welcome. But you *will* remove the Dowager Duchess from the list, do you hear me?"

She heaved a rebellious sigh. "Sebastian, I insist…"

"You…*insist?*"

Her heart thumped painfully against her ribcage. The

look of warning he gave her sent a rash of goose bumps rippling over her arms. His eyes were as filled with ice as the winter lakes.

"Sebastian," she murmured shakily, "please tell me. I can see whatever it is upse—"

"The subject of the Dowager Duchess is closed, Jocelyn," he gritted out. "You will never mention her name in this house again, and you are forbidden from having any contact with her whatsoever. Do you understand me?"

"You cannot forbid me this without an explanation, Sebastian. Make me understand."

"You will obey me in this matter, Jocelyn," he ordered.

She gaped at him. "You are being insufferable. I will not listen to such nonsense without an explanation. She is a part of our family, Sebastian."

His hands reached out for her, but he halted himself and only choked the air with a furious expression on his face. Jocelyn's eyes widened, she could not help feel as if he would dearly love to have his hands around her neck. He seemed to rein in his emotions and his hand circled her neck, his thumb caressing her lower lip. His touch was gentle, but there was steel behind it.

"It is not wise to willfully disobey my wishes, my duchess."

Ire spiked through her. "Do you plan to strangle me, then, as you did your mistress, if I do not obey?" she spat out, angered that he was not willing to talk to her.

Regret sliced through her the instant she released the words. He dropped his hands as if he had been stung, which she supposed he had. She flinched from the look in his eyes. She had thought him cold and remote before, but it was as if he became the very god of ice and snow.

"Forgive me!" she rasped.

She waited in the tense silence for him to apologize in return. Or say something. Anything.

But he ignored her completely as he methodically dressed and reached for his cloak.

"Are you leaving?" she cried.

Shame burned through her. How *could* she have thrown that foul rumor in his face? It was unconscionable, even if he had upset her with his barely commands.

She grasped his arm, "Sebastian, please let us talk."

He offered nothing, no assurances or explanations, merely yanked his arm free from her grasp.

A sick feeling grew in the pit of her stomach as he pivoted and stalked out, slamming the door behind him without uttering another word.

. . .

The arctic chill at Sherring Cross had more to do with the total silence between Jocelyn and Sebastian than the winter snow that fell so steadily outside.

She did not know how to reach him. He had withdrawn completely, brooding and spending his entire days locked in his study. What tormented her even more was that he did not respond to her overtures of peace, nor did he take her in his arms at night. She had slept restlessly for the past week, desperately wanting him, helpless against his wall of distant reserve. Nothing thawed him. He was chillingly polite when he spoke. Their conversations were confined to the mundane, and Jocelyn despaired of ever finding a way to breach his solid wall. The aloof courtesy he treated her with left her baffled.

Desperate to distract herself from her unhappiness, lest she go mad, she had thrown all her energy into planning the holiday dinner.

Within days, she had turned the mausoleum of an estate into a cozy home. Rooms where Sebastian had forbidden the fireplaces to be lighted, she had ordered to be cleaned, and now they smelled of fresh lemons and pine. Fires roared and crackled, and the cold, dank feel of the place gradually warmed under her careful ministrations and strict orders.

Miniature incandescent lamps dotted the mantels, and were used to light the towering Christmas tree in the great room. Red drapes were added to the silver ones. Pine cones, evergreens, and mistletoe decorated nearly every room. Slowly the mansion transcended beauty under her touch. She was awed as she toured the rooms with Mrs. Otterbsy, admiring the fruit of their days of relentless work.

Restless energy ate a Jocelyn. Several of her gowns had already arrived from London, along with the gifts she had ordered for her family. The milliner in the village had been in rapture when she came in and opened an account, ordering several gifts for the twins and her sisters. She had ordered Sebastian's special gift from Mr. Wallaby, at a shop in upper Lincolnshire that specialized in antiquities. When she had first seen the green jade dragon it had reminded her of Sebastian. She hoped he would love it, but most of all she prayed that the silence between them would end before their Christmas dinner—just seven days away.

The worst was, she feared she was in love with him.

A bleak smile played over her lips. It was irrational to feel fear upon realizing that she loved someone other than her sisters, brother, and father. That she loved her husband. It was such a different kind of love, intense and deep, filling her with a longing to be with him always.

She knew she would tell him, and soon. She wanted only honesty between them, even though her heart ached with the knowledge that he could not possibly feel the same about her. If he did, he would not be shutting her out, hiding from her whatever it was that tormented him so.

She had seen the flash of rage just before he closed himself off when she mentioned his mother the first time, though there were times when she wondered if she had only imagined it. She despaired even more as she recalled his response to her blunder about a mistress.

She wrung her hands, frantic to find a way to break the silence. A thought stormed through her.

What if she revealed her feelings to him?

Would he then be more open? What if he was so withdrawn only because he thought she believed the rumors?

She swallowed and made up her mind. She was not afraid to confess her love. And what could it hurt? She hurried to his study, knocked, and entered before he bid her go away.

He glanced up at her intrusion, and his raw beauty warmed her as always. Garbed in gray trousers with a snow white shirt with the sleeves rolled up to his elbow, he appeared relaxed and at home. Unfortunately, he seemed so cold and frighteningly unapproachable that he scared her.

"How my I assist you, Jocelyn?"

His polite inquiry was so bland she almost changed her mind. The vulnerability felt terrible. But she took a breath and stated the truth.

"I am in love with you."

She met his gaze, and leaned against the closed door. Her hands were clasped so tightly around the handle that she knew she'd have welts on her palm.

When he did not respond, only stared at her with his icy blues, she repeated, "I am in love with you, Sebastian. I love you. Your warmth, your generosity with your tenants, your intensity…your passion. Your—"

"Enough, madam!" he bit out.

She could feel his fury pouring over her in waves. What had she said to make his eyes fill with such anger?

"I neither want nor require your love, Jocelyn. Do not speak such things." His admonishment whipped over her, stinging and flaying.

"You are angry because I love you?" She did not think it possible for his expression to become more closed off, but it did.

"Did you not hear when I just ordered you not to speak to me of such things?" His voice had grown so forbidding she hesitated, her natural boldness squelched under the utter disdain that flowed from him.

"I love you, Sebastian. You not wanting to hear it won't stop it from being true. I am not asking you to return the sentiment. I will not say it again if that is your desire, but know that every time I look at you, touch you, kiss you, and when you are deep inside me and I am calling out your name, I am saying I love you. That is, if you ever return to our bed."

She did not wait for a response, or even watch his reaction. She whirled and jerked the door open, and stalked from the room.

She feared he would never come back to her, no matter how hard she tried.

• • •

Sebastian was rooted to his chair. Her words washed over him and punched into a deep, cold recess in his heart. He felt a crack, and hardened himself at the rush of feelings. It could not have been easy for her to declare herself in the face of his indifference.

"I do not believe Jocelyn was aware that I was in the room."

At Anthony's amazed remark, Sebastian swiveled in his chair to face his brother. He had arrived early for the Christmas gathering, and Sebastian had yet to inform her.

"I don't think I have ever seen you looking quite so at a loss, Sebastian." Anthony grinned at the scowl that Sebastian sent him.

"Shut up, damn it," he snapped, and prowled over to the decanter to pour two whiskeys. "How is Phillipa?" he asked as he handed one to his brother.

"Very happy and contented. She will journey down with her sisters and parents in a couple of days." Anthony took a healthy swallow of his drink. "I thought someone was playing a prank when I read in *The Times* that you had wed Lady Jocelyn Rathbourne. Then I realized it must be true, because who would dare?"

Sebastian grunted, and stalked to the windows. He opened them a crack, letting in the chill.

"Bloody hell, Sebastian, you and the damn cold!" Anthony rose and joined him, gazing out at the landscape that was blanketed white with snow. "How on earth did it come about that you married Lady Jocelyn?"

Sebastian ground his teeth. "She barged in here with a derringer, claiming you had taken advantage of her and demanding satisfaction."

"The hell you say!"

Sebastian broke down and chuckled as amusement trickled through him. "She was quite amazing. And I thought that instead of choosing one of the vapid, shallow misses who pepper the *ton*, a bold and adventurous woman would be preferable. Although I've come to realize that my days would be far more peaceful with a more biddable wife."

He glanced at his brother, and they both roared with laughter. It was the first time he'd cracked a smile in days.

"I don't think I have ever seen you this surprised, Anthony."

"Lord. I knew the woman was fearless, but I never thought she would appear on your doorstep with a gun, Sebastian! Good God, man!" Anthony thrust his hands through the blond hair that fell in wild disarray, so different from the severe cut he normally wore.

"I was a bit taken aback myself," he admitted with a reluctant grin.

Green eyes so different from his own assessed him. "And then you wed her without knowing if I had been with her as she'd claimed?"

Sebastian heard the undisguised shock in his brother's question. "Whatever you are Anthony, is not the libertine she claimed. I knew something must have happened or she would not have had Mother's locket in her possession. But I did not believe you capable of betraying Phillipa so completely—not when you had been making such an ass of yourself." Sebastian sipped his whiskey.

Anthony winced. "Bloody hell."

Sebastian said nothing, just downed the rest of his whiskey.

His brother jetted out a breath. "I went to Lincolnshire to gain some perspective, and Jocelyn came out of nowhere. I thought I desired her, and kissed her a few times, but nothing beyond that, Sebastian. Her beauty was so different from Phillipa's, and her character, as well. I became enchanted. And of course there was her pedigree— I believed I was making the right decision."

"Why did you change your mind?" Sebastian asked, and waited patiently while Anthony poured another whiskey.

"She scared me."

Sebastian gave a bark of laughter.

"It's no laughing matter, Sebastian." Anthony grimaced in chagrin. "She rode her horse astride, her skills with her bow surpassed any I had ever seen. She *hunted*, Sebastian. And I don't mean for fox. After a few weeks, I realized how different she was from the women of the *ton*. She made no effort to be demure, and her energy left me dizzy. It had enticed me to think she would make a bloody awesome bed partner—" He broke off at the glare Sebastian sent him, and shrugged. "I'm just telling you my thoughts at the time. But it was mostly the lure of Phillipa that drew me away."

"Just take care," Sebastian said evenly. "Did you propose?"

"No," Anthony said softly. "But I meant for my actions to be interpreted as such. Phillipa had rejected my offer of marriage and I was reeling. Jocelyn and I became friends and I knew she needed to make her estate solvent. I left the locket with her and returned to London to ensure Phillipa was not with child before I made any concrete decisions in relation to her. You know all that happened after."

"I see," Sebastian said.

Anthony jerked his chin at the study door. "What was that all about? Her comment about you being absent from her bed?"

Sebastian related the gist of their fight in a cold, clipped voice.

Anthony lifted a bemused brow. "She has heard the rumors about Marissa? Have you explained?"

"What is there to explain?" Sebastian ground out. "I have no desire to dredge up my past mistakes."

"Jocelyn is your duchess, Sebastian. Do you think the old rumors won't surface upon her first foray to London? Don't be blind, man. Many will flock to her side wanting to be associated with you, and there will always be those who thrive on gossip and innuendo, if not outright lies. And really, it is hardly fair to expect her to obey you about Mother without questioning your reasons."

Sebastian stared at him intently. "Are you saying Phillipa would gainsay your wishes?"

Anthony gazed out at the falling snow. "No, but, I assure you, their temperaments are very different. Besides, I tell my wife the reasons behind my decisions."

Sebastian threw back the rest of his whiskey. "I do not speak of our mother."

"Will you ever forgive her? She longs for you, Sebastian, she—"

"Enough!" Sebastian gritted his teeth and slowly unclenched his hands from his glass, fearing it will crack. "I said I will not discuss our mother. Not even with you, Anthony. I do not give a damn what she longs for," he snarled, and prowled the study with restless energy. "And when my duchess enters society, I have no fear that she will handle herself brilliantly."

"She will. Even in the short time we have been acquainted, I know her to be fearless and poised."

Sebastian grunted in agreement.

"Have you read the remainder of Mother's journals?"

"You know I have not," he ground out. "I will not discuss her further, Anthony."

"I read them in one sitting, Sebastian, and you refuse to hear about its contents from me. I believe if you were to read all twelve volumes you would not feel such disdain for her."

Sebastian glanced at his brother with blank eyes. "I will not discuss this further, Anthony."

"Well, then," Anthony murmured, stuck his hand in his trouser pocket, and bounced on his toes a couple of times. The seconds drew out until he said, "So, I see Jocelyn has been busy decorating for the festive season. The place fairly glows."

"I noticed," Sebastian clipped out as he rolled down his sleeves and reached for his riding jacket. "Let's visit the stables. Further talk of Jocelyn's avowal and our mother are off limits."

He ignored his brother's taunting chuckle as they strode outside into the bracing cold. He hoped the cold would help harden him against the rush of emotions he had been feeling since Jocelyn's heartfelt declaration.

He had not let himself be open to love for years. Not since Marissa's perfidy. Sweet words and coyly delivered promises of love sickened him.

As he stalked toward the stables, he thought about how his wife had declared herself. There had been nothing sweet, or shy, or remotely coy about it.

His duchess had been bold and unflinching, true to her temperament.

And he had been a complete bastard.

• • •

JUNE 19ᵀᴴ 1864

TODAY IS SEBASTIAN'S TWELFTH BIRTHDAY CELEBRATION. I HAVE BEEN ORDERED TO NOT BE THERE. I DEEPLY WISH I COULD, BUT I KNOW THAT CLEMENT WILL EXECUTE HIS THREAT TO BANISH ME FROM SHERRING CROSS IF I DO NOT ADHERE TO HIS DEMANDS. THERE ARE TIMES I THINK BANISHMENT WOULD BE PREFERABLE TO THE COLD SILENCE I MUST ENDURE. I HAVE TRIED IN SO MANY WAYS TO CONNECT WITH MY BEAUTIFUL BOY BUT HE ONLY STARES AT ME WITH HATRED. HOW I WISH I COULD HUG HIM TO ME, AND TELL HIM HOW MUCH I LOVE HIM, AND HOW PROUD I AM OF HIM. MY HEART SHATTERED AS I—

Sebastian closed the journal softly and leaned back in the sofa, his heart squeezing.

After deeply contemplating Anthony's stance on how Sebastian treated his duchess and their mother, he had approached reading the rest of his mother's diaries with a calm stoicism he had not expected himself to possess.

Slowly, as he'd read the heart-wrenching words of his young mother, his hatred had tempered and his condemnation thawed. Some semblance of regret had sliced through him, deep and painful. He'd then felt consumed with the need to learn everything about her. Hours passed as he absorbed her words, the crackling of the fire the only sound in the library.

It was through the lines of her diaries, absorbing the

passion, the love, the unending need and warmth she derived from her lover, which caused the first pulse of need for more in his life to flare within Sebastian. He had been utterly shocked to realize that he was lonely. He realized how cold and withdrawn he was from everything around him, especially from Jocelyn. He had shuttered himself away from his wife in the same manner his father had done with his mother, and yet, Jocelyn deserved none of his anger.

He was grateful for the small measure of peace he found from the hurt and betrayals of his childhood. He understood some of the pain she'd had to endure being kept away from him. He had always thought she'd chosen to stay away, being too consumed with her lover. But it had been his father's way of punishing her for her unfaithfulness. Had he known he was punishing Sebastian, as well?

He glanced down at the volume gripped in his hand. She'd written that she loved him wholeheartedly. Her accounts of his many accomplishments and her overwhelming pride in him were unmistakable, even to his biased eyes.

He had six more journals to read. He knew Jocelyn needed to understand his refusal to have his mother at Sherring Cross, and he would explain. But Sebastian still doubted he could have his mother's presence in his home so soon. He understood her need for her lover, but he still had not forgiven her for it.

His mind shifted to Jocelyn, and his heart became quiet. He thought about the words his duchess had so passionately declared, and an ache settled deep inside him. He could imagine what his silence and coldness must have done to her. He could not escape the knowledge that the past few weeks with her had been the most blissful time of his life.

She loved him. But did he love her? He still doubted he had the capacity to accept and give love. Love was something he had banished from his life years ago out of necessity, but she made him yearn to be loved. That passion his mother wrote about. The need to share, to be comforted, and the joys that are found in laughter. He found it all in Jocelyn. The days of silence had been hell, and he admired the strength it had taken for her to admit that she loved him. The ache in his chest was almost unbearable.

He had the urge to go to her and explain his actions, but he repressed the feelings for now. He himself did not fully understand. He had much to atone for with his duchess, but allowing his mother to visit so soon, Sebastian could not grant her. His wound felt too raw. She would have to allow him to reconcile in his own time. His headstrong duchess would have to concede to his wishes on this, at least.

Chapter Eight

I THANK YOU, LADY JOCELYN, FOR YOUR WARM GREETINGS. VISCOUNT RADCLIFFE AND I ARE MUCH HONORED TO ACCEPT YOUR INVITATION TO CHRISTMAS DINNER. I AM SO VERY THANKFUL THAT SEBASTIAN IS HAPPY TO HAVE US IN HIS HOME, ALTHOUGH I CONFESS TO BEING A BIT SURPRISED. BUT MOST PLEASANTLY SO, I ASSURE YOU. I AM LOOKING FORWARD TO MAKING YOUR ACQUAINTANCE.

YOURS,

MARGARET, LADY RADCLIFFE

Sebastian's mother.

Jocelyn had blatantly disobeyed him and invited the woman to the Christmas gathering.

The rage that gripped him unnerved even Sebastian himself.

He read the note for the fifth time, still in disbelief. It had been by pure chance that he had stumbled upon it. He had seen the seal and recognized it as his mother's lover's seal. So he had opened it, despite its being addressed to Jocelyn. He could not believe the nerve of the woman.

He realized that he had been too soft on his wife, allowing her far too much latitude. Something had to be done.

He summoned her to his study, and sat down to wait.

She swept into his domain looking glorious as usual, and he girded himself against the desire that flooded through him. Her hair was upswept in the most severe fashion, but the tendrils that curled loosely over her forehead softened the effect. The purple tea gown she wore bared the creamy swell of her breasts and Sebastian itched to pull her into his lap and have his way with them.

"You summoned me, Your Grace?"

He could see the wariness in her eyes. Three days had passed since her declaration of love and he had ignored her completely, not even dining with her. He had needed the distance so he could think clearly. So he could come to peace with all he'd learned about his mother, and unravel why Jocelyn's words would affect him so. And then this.

She did not understand the full extent of the trouble she was in.

He smiled, but not pleasantly. "Do you have something to tell me, Jocelyn?" He kept his voice deliberately bland, lest he bellow his rage.

"I do not, Sebastian."

He surged to his feet and stalked around his desk to lean against it. "I detest liars. Have I not made myself clear on that regard?"

Puzzlement shadowed her face as she took two halting steps forward. "I have not lied to you, Sebastian."

"Then how would you explain this, madam?" He pushed the note forward, and it fluttered to the ground.

She stooped to pick it up. "Oh!" She gasped as she read the contents. Sebastian blinked in disbelief when she had the nerve to smile broadly at him. "I was not sure if she would respond."

He wondered if she was daft. "How is it that you fail to understand your precarious position…" he murmured softly. Then roared, "You defied me!"

Her body jumped, startled at his anger. "You gave me no choice," she snapped. "I had no way of reaching you, Sebastian. There has been tension between us for ten bloody days. I have tried in so many ways to mend my thoughtless remark, to explain my feelings, but you have shut me out completely."

"So you sought to manipulate me by inviting my mother after I have forbidden it?" he asked incredulously. "You have not comprehended your folly, madam. As you so indelicately pointed out, the last woman that tried to manipulate me is dead."

"I did not try to manipulate you!" She clutched her hands and glared at him. "I wanted to provoke a reaction from you. And I succeeded. Your anger is better by far than the icy detachment you have thus far treated me to."

"Do you believe so, madam?" he said with chilling softness. "You will retract your invitation, Jocelyn, and you will do so immediately."

She glared at him mutinously. "I will not. If you will but hear me out—"

"There is nothing to hear, Jocelyn. Retract the invitation immediately."

"I will not!"

He clenched his teeth, debating how to deal with this…this…flagrant insubordination. It wasn't so much the invitation that infuriated him as her blatant, willful defiance of his orders. "Where have you been living, Jocelyn?"

"What do you mean?" She sent him a baffled glance.

"Where have you been residing for the past twenty years? Has it been in Lincolnshire, England?"

"I do not understand what your questions have to do with our discussion, but yes."

"Let me educate you, then. You are my wife. Thus, my property. I am well within my rights to beat you if I so desire, or banish you from my sight. I am trying to understand how you thought you could so blatantly defy me and go unpunished. I believe the best punishment will be to banish you. To Devonshire. And it would be an injustice if I did not beat you first."

Her jaw dropped in outrage. "You arrogant, egotistical, unfeeling *beast*!"

She launched herself at him.

Her actions so surprised him, he did not brace to check her momentum.

"*Oomph.*"

Her muffled scream as she slammed into him had him letting out a laugh in amazed disbelief. But it was quickly wiped away as her palm swung and caught him solidly on the cheek.

Good God. He had truly enraged his duchess. Was she really not aware that he would never beat her? He doubted he had the heart to banish her from his sight, either.

"You do not display much prudence, do you, wife?"

Her breaths heaved, making the swell of her breasts rise precariously above the gown. Her eyes darkened to almost black as they glared a furious dare at him.

Just that quickly, he wanted her. A fierce need to possess her surged through him. And not in the slow and languid way of their nights of loving before their falling out.

He needed her. And he wanted her to burn.

• • •

Sebastian's mouth crashed down on Jocelyn's, stunning her at the abrupt turn of his mood.

The intensity of his mouth as it captured hers sent shocks of desire through her whole body. She responded with complete hunger, gripping his dark head tightly to her.

"Oh, yes!" she gasped as he roughly yanked down the bodice of her gown, as though its low cut had been fashioned exactly for his ravishment. His lips covered her pebbled nipple.

"Sebastian," she cried out.

He stalked backward with her, whipping up the hem of her dress and petticoats, pushing the layers of fabric upward as he trailed his hands up her legs. She gasped into the mouth that kissed her as the back of her knees hit his oak desk. Papers and objects flew, and he lifted her bottom onto the desk. His breath was ragged as he withdrew his mouth from hers and stepped between her thighs, wedging them apart and hoisting her legs to his waist. Then his fingers deftly parted her bloomers, exposing her to the chilly air.

That, and the scalding look of passion on his face sent erotic shivers dancing up her spine.

"You infuriate me," he growled. "I do not know if I should beat you, strangle you, or kiss you."

"Do I have a say?" she managed breathily.

His jaw worked as he pulled his member from his trousers. "No."

Then he angled her hips up and slammed into her in one powerful movement.

The desk jerked. Her scream of pleasure-pain rang in the library. He kissed her brutally before withdrawing and forging home again, slower, but just as powerfully.

"You also drive me mad," he all but snarled as he gripped her hair, then feasted on her lips again.

Jocelyn reeled with pleasure at the intensity of his lovemaking. It had never been like this before, his control shattered. Weakness infused her limbs, and dark, wanton need seared through her. She tried to rise to meet his thrusts, but with the powerful grip he had on her hips she couldn't move. She could only submit to his powerful strokes and the merciless pleasure that he rained upon her. He buried his face in the curve of her neck as his hips plunged faster, driving into her over and over, hard and relentless, sending deep shards of pleasure to her very core. She felt his teeth at her shoulder, scraping against her skin, nipping her with erotic bites. Burning ecstasy speared her body, and she came apart in a thousand pieces.

He plunged once more into her convulsing body, and with a harsh roar he tumbled with her, emptying his essence into her.

"My God, Sebastian," she gasped long moments later, still trembling from the aftershocks of such violent pleasure.

He groaned against her lips before capturing them in a kiss that only served to make her mindless. "I cannot believe I have been absent from your bed for ten days."

Hope surged through Jocelyn.

"Does that mean I will not be beaten or banished?" she asked breathlessly as he lifted and carried her, still impaled, over to the sofa. She moaned at the sensations that traveled through her at the feel of him hardening inside her again. He sat on the sofa with her straddling him, the skirt of her gown spilling backward over his knees, his morning coat crushed beneath her folded legs and bunched-up petticoats.

"You infuriate me, Jocelyn, but know that I would never lift a hand to hurt you in any way."

"Banishment, then?"

He grunted and her heart raced at his intent regard.

"I do not have a pleasant relationship with my mother," he said without preamble. "It has been so since I found her with her lover in the gardens when I was six."

Jocelyn stiffened in shock. "Oh, Sebastian, I'm—"

He shook his head to cut her off. "The rift only got worse after she married her lover, Lord Radcliffe, only three months after my father's passing."

Regret flooded through her, as it dawned what she had done by sending that invitation. No wonder he was furious. "Oh, husband, I am so sorry. If I'd known—"

"I had planned on explaining everything to you tonight. I realized what an ass I have been for not speaking to you as I tried to come to grips with how you make me feel. It was wrong, and I'm sorry for that."

She blinked, her heart stalling with dread. "H-how do I make you feel?"

"Be silent and listen, Jocelyn." He nipped at her lips. "You came into my life and completely turned it upside down, when all I wanted was a biddable wife to give me an heir."

All the hope she'd felt a moment ago fled in an instant, and a noise of anguish escaped her throat.

He didn't love her. He would get her with child, and then he would banish her, just as he'd threatened. Oh, God, what had she done?

• • •

Sebastian cursed as Jocelyn stiffened, her muscles tightening, sending shards of pleasure running along his cock, still buried deep inside her. Then she squirmed, attempting to climb off him and get away.

"Be still!" he rasped, his fingers digging into her hips.

"No! I—"

He gave her a shake. "Just listen, damn you!"

He groaned as she wriggled, settling closer on his lap, loving the rush of liquid heat from her, telling him how much she wanted him.

But he needed to finish this conversation before giving in to the arousal. He gripped her hips and gently eased her off him. He grunted at the sensations that travelled through him as her tight clasp reluctantly released him. He tucked himself back into his trousers and drew her down on his lap. He held her chin gently and titled her face up to meet his gaze.

She froze, her eyes questioning, and he went on before she could move. "When you stormed my library, so fearless and demanding, I knew immediately. It was you I wanted, not some vapid miss without a thought in her head."

He felt her rigid muscles relax a little.

"Truthfully, never did I expect you to enthrall me as you have. The days I spent with you only carried me further and further into my feelings for you, and I began to fear your lure. I withdrew, uncomfortable with the intensity of my emotions. The last time I felt anything close to this, I fought a duel over a married woman…whom society still believes I murdered."

"Oh!" Her uncertain gaze shifted to disconcerted.

"But what I feel for you is wholly different. You make me burn with life, and yearn to set aside my cold and distant, solitary ways."

"Oh, Sebastian." Her eyes softened with love, and she tenderly kissed his face and his lips.

"I am not finished, Jocelyn," he murmured between kisses. "We will not have this conversation again, so I implore you to be attentive."

She gave him a radiant smile and stilled.

"I had already decided to break the silence with my mother after reading a series of her journals. I may not fully understand what she did, but I can empathize with her plight, and the agony she felt over her decisions. But reaching out to her was something I wanted to do on my own terms."

Jocelyn lowered her eyes, toying with the buttons of his shirt. "Can you ever forgive me? I—"

"I know you are not repentant, Jocelyn," he said wryly.

Her contrite expression melted into a mischievous smile, and Sebastian embraced the notion that for some mysterious reason, her disobedience no longer bothered him.

"When you foray into society as my duchess you will hear many things whispered, and I do not want you to be ambushed. Marissa was my lover both before and after she was married. In a bid to force my hand, she accepted the offer from an earl, hoping that jealously would bring me up to scratch. It did not."

He grimaced. He had been determined never to marry. Ironically, that had led him into exactly the same situation for which he'd always condemned his mother. He just hadn't seen that until now.

"I foolishly continued the affair," he went on. "Marissa wanted me badly enough that she told me lies of her husband's brutal beatings, hoping I would call him out and kill him." He swallowed, hating the memories of that time. "As proof, she showed me horrible bruises, which I later learned were self-inflicted. And I fell for it. I challenged her husband to a duel, which he accepted eagerly." Sebastian traced a finger over the scar on his cheek. "He gave me this, and I almost killed him."

Jocelyn's eyes were wide with dismay. "That's awful," she murmured.

"As he lay wounded and cursing, I realized he believed it was me abusing his wife so viciously. She'd been lying to both of us. I confronted her, and she confessed she'd done it to be free to wed me. She implored me to actually kill him so we could be together. Of course I wouldn't, and ended our association. She threatened to kill herself because she loved me so desperately. When I ignored her threats, she later hanged herself. Then the foul rumors surfaced that I strangled her."

Jocelyn's face went ashen. "Little wonder you do not want

to hear my words of love."

He gently captured her lips. "No, you're wrong. I've changed. Because of you. I want the kind of marriage you once described to me. To communicate, and share, and make decisions together"

Slowly, her face cleared, and her lips parted. "I do believe you love me, Sebastian," she said, her eyes filled with wonder.

Warmth unfurled through his whole body, and intense love filled his heart to bursting.

He gripped her hips, spinning and tumbling her into the depths of the sofa. He settled between her thighs and kissed her lips with tenderness. "I believe I do, my duchess, I do believe I love you."

• • •

Christmas Day

Fierce pride and joy filled Jocelyn as she looked around the massive dining table. It was perfect. Everyone had arrived, and laugher and merriment spilled through the halls of Sherring Cross.

The parlor rang with excited chatter from her father, brother and sisters, Anthony and Phillipa, Phillipa's sister and parents, and the dowager Duchess Margaret, Sebastian's mother, with her lord, and Sebastian's sister Constance. Jocelyn had expected the dowager to be cold and forbidding, but the dainty creature that looked up at her long-lost son with such wide, imploring eyes had surprised her. Sebastian had not disappointed, and Margaret and Jocelyn both had been pleased with their first tentative conversation.

She and Victoria had been gratified and a little bemused at the twins' shrieks of joy to be dining at the table with the adults. They had all crooned over the roast ducks, turkeys, stuffed pigeons, and roasted pork. Not to mention the

Christmas pudding and punch.

Jocelyn could not have asked for a more perfect day.

She thought of her mama, and emotions tightened her throat. How she wished Mama could be here! How she would have loved it all.

Sebastian's gaze met hers, and she gave him a smile and a subtle signal, then swept out of the room, away from the bustle. She went into the library, the room she thought of as their special place. All the things that brought them together so deliciously had happened there.

She stood at his favorite window, staring out at the snow falling steadily over the estate that she had come to love as home. Excitement bubbled through her.

His strong hands curved around her waist and he held her from behind. "Do you wish to retire?" he murmured, kissing her nape.

"I doubt they would forgive us." She smiled at his reflection in the frosty window pane. "I have a gift for you."

His brows went up, but he looked pleased. "Another?"

"Yes, I thought I should tell you tonight, considering the multitude of generous gifts that you have showered on me."

"Tell me what?"

She spun in the circle of his strong arms, glowing with joy and contentment. "Our child will be here in the summer."

"Our—"

The stunned look of elation on his face made her heart overflow with love. "Merry Christmas, my love."

Sebastian wrapped her in his arms and held her tight. "And Merry Christmas to you, my sweet duchess. You've made me the happiest man in the world."

Acknowledgments

This would not have been possible without the blessings and favour of God. To my husband Dusean, whom I adore. Thank you for being my biggest fan and supporter, and for loving the fact that I am a ninja in disguise. To my sisters, Hayley Lawrence and Kadia Hufford, thank you for rooting for me, and just for being awesome.

To my amazing editor Nina Bruhns, for enjoying my characters as much as I do, being challenging yet supportive, and just fabulous to work with!

To Tanesha Westcarr, for being encouraging when I had self-doubts. To my beta readers, Cadian Drummond, Chaday Taylor Nelson, Diedre Mcleod, and Elrona Gooden, for reading my first, second, and third drafts!

Thank you!

About the Author

I am an avid reader of novels with a deep passion for writing. I especially love romance and adore writing about people falling in love. I live a lot in the worlds I create and I actively speak to my characters (out loud). I have a warrior way "never give up on my dream." When I am not writing, I spend a copious amount of time drooling over Rick Grimes from *Walking Dead*, watching Japanese Anime and playing video games with my love—Dusean Nelson. I have a horrible weakness for ice cream.

I am always happy to hear from readers and would love for you to connect with me via Website | Faceook | Twitter

For sneak peeks on my upcoming books, excerpts, general speak on hot guys, kick ass heroines, and romance titbits, join me in The Riot.

Happy reading!

Get Scandalous with these historical reads...

THE EARL'S RETURN
a *Marriage Mart Mayhem* novel by Callie Hutton

At first, Lady Mary doesn't recognize Lord Redgrave as the cad who ran out on her sister two weeks before their wedding. After giving him the cut direct in a London ballroom, she finds herself running into him everywhere she goes, and fighting a forbidden at-traction. Redgrave means to stay away from Mary but it is impos-sible. Not only has Mary sworn off men, Redgrave is so very wrong for her. But she cannot stop thinking of his kisses. Passion between two people who can never be together is a dangerous game.

REAL EARLS BREAK THE RULES
an *Infamous Somertons* novel by Tina Gabrielle

Brandon St. Clair, the Earl of Vale, has never been one to follow the rules. Even though he must marry a wealthy heiress so that he can be rid of the pile of debt he inherited with his title, he can't stop thinking of another. Amelia Somerton is the daughter of a forger and is *not* a suitable wife. But that doesn't stop Brandon from making Amelia a different offer, the kind that breaks every rule of etiquette... But what begins as a simple arrangement, soon escalates into much more, and as the heat between them sizzles, each encounter becomes a lesson in seduction.

His Lordship's Wild Highland Bride

a *Those Magnificent Malverns* novel by Kathleen Bittner Roth

Ridley Malvern, Lord Caulfield, desperate for a dowry, agrees to marry a wealthy Scot's daughter sight unseen. All Lainie MacGregor desires is to return to her clan. Attempting to make things right, Caulfield takes Lainie back to the Highlands only to discover that his wife is wanted for murder. For her safekeeping, they must remain in England. Now Ridley needs to win her affections and prove that a wild Highland lass and an English lord, can find a love match, after all.

The Wager

a *Sisters of Scandal* novel by Lily Maxton

Anne Middleton never plays by the rules. She is willful when she should be obedient and unabashed when she should be decorous. Worse still, she can never resist a good wager. Michael Grey—the Earl of Thornhill—knows Anne is no lady of decorum, but her bold impulsiveness slips through his armor, and propriety is forgotten. Roused by heady desire, Michael tempts Anne in a way she cannot resist—a wager. Thus begins a game of chance, where coins have been replaced by a currency that is far more illicit. And the stakes of seduction are dangerous indeed...

Made in the USA
Las Vegas, NV
26 October 2021